Battle Creek

Battle Creek

A Tale of Slavery and Freedom in Colonial Maryland

Neil Didriksen

CITYLIT
PRESS

Baltimore, Maryland

Library of Congress Control Number: 2012956265

ISBN: 978-1-936328-12-3

CityLit Project is a 501(c)(3) nonprofit organization
with offices in the School of Communications Design
at the University of Baltimore.

Federal Tax ID Number: 20-0639118

Printed in the United States of America | First Edition

Cover and Interior Illustrations: Tom Chalkley

Editorial Assistant: Ashley Payne

Book Design: Gregg Wilhelm

CITYLIT
PRESS

c/o CityLit Project

120 S. Curley Street

Baltimore, MD 21224

410.274.5691

www.CityLitProject.org

info@citylitproject.org

To my parents, Erika and Mathias, who traveled to these shores as teenagers, found each other, and started our family's American story and journey.

Colonial Maryland

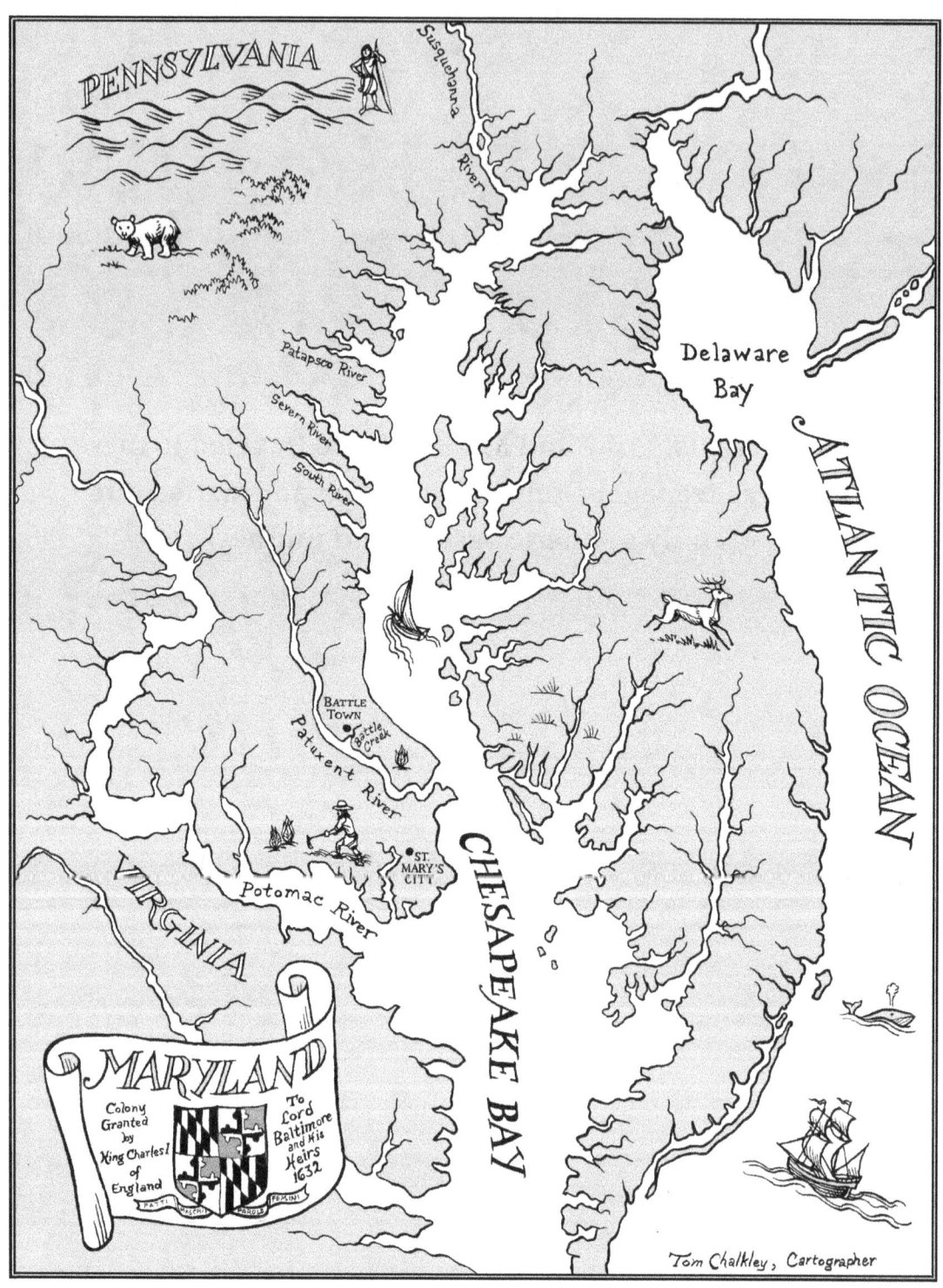

Tom Chalkley, Cartographer

Contents

Spring 1672

Spring 1673

Continued...

Spring 1674

Spring, 1675

1

Coming Ashore

SPRING 1672 — Paul stood on the empty deck of the *Providence*, at anchor in the calm, clear waters of Battle Creek. He shivered slightly in the light spring breeze blowing across the water. After months at sea, he was ready to leave the ship and follow Rebecca, his 11-year-old sister, and Captain Darby into the skiff that would carry them ashore.

But memories held him on deck. His mind was back in the terrible storm that had taken his father's life. He felt the pain that seized his body when he realized his father was gone. Unlike Rebecca, he had not cried. At 14, he wouldn't allow himself to cry. He was the head of their family. He had to be strong. He had to take care of his sister. But how? How would they survive in this place called Maryland?

He hated the *Providence* and the sadness it had brought to their lives. Yet the ship seemed safe compared to this strange, new land and the future before them.

"Paul," called Captain Darby, "there're men waiting for us on shore."

Determined to put the past behind them, Paul climbed down the ladder into the skiff where his sister was sitting next to Darby. As two sailors rowed them away from the *Providence*, Paul kept his arm tightly around Rebecca. He could feel her trembling through her light coat. She'd been afraid ever since the storm. Many nights Paul would wake to hear her crying. He had hoped she'd improve once they left the ship. Now he wasn't sure.

As soon as the skiff reached the wharf, Captain Darby rose and quickly climbed up the ladder. "Follow me," he called back to Paul and Rebecca.

Paul reached for their small bundle of worn, dirty clothes and climbed up after Darby. With his feet on the wharf, he turned to help Rebecca. But the first mate already had lifted her gently out of the skiff. Then the mate gave a rough shove to McNeely, the other passenger, whose iron chains struck against the wooden rungs as he climbed up the ladder.

Captain Darby already was moving with his usual rapid strides down the wharf. Paul reached for Rebecca's hand and hurried to catch up, almost dragging her behind him.

"This is Battle Town on Battle Creek," said Darby, "your new home."

Home sounded good to Paul. With their father dead, a home is what he needed for Rebecca. But this place called Battle Town was nothing like their home in England. Paul could see fewer than a half-dozen buildings scattered around the open fields carved out of the thick, dark forest. All the buildings were wood. Most were tiny and dreary. There were no shops, no roads, no wagons or carts. There was no noise. Something's missing, thought Paul. Where are the women and children?

Captain Darby caught the surprised look on Paul's face. "It may not seem like much to you, young Paul, but Battle Town is the center of life in this part of the colony."

"But it's so small and empty!"

"I've carried over 120 men to these shores in the past eight years. Those who survived now live up and down Battle Creek. They grow some of the best tobacco you'll find on the Chesapeake."

"Who lives here in Battle Town?"

"That large house belongs to Michael Taney. He holds 3,000 acres on this side of Battle Creek and has more than twenty men working his fields. Thomas Cosgrove owns the other large building, the Punch, which is the only inn in this region."

Paul still had his doubts. The inn and the house were rough looking structures, with only a few, tiny windows facing out toward the water and odd-looking chimneys poking up through their roofs. The other buildings looked more like sheds and shacks. Giant oaks and beech trees surrounded the town like an impenetrable wall. They were taller than any he had seen in England. Sunlight didn't penetrate through their dense branches and leaves, making the forest appear dark and dangerous.

"Captain Darby," called a lean and well-dressed man standing in front of the inn, "we've been expecting you for a fortnight. We began to think you'd forgotten about us."

"No, Mister Taney," replied Darby respectfully, "I didn't forget you. But three days out of Barbados, we were struck by a fierce storm."

Taney cast a suspicious eye toward Darby. He didn't trust these sea captains. They charged him too much for the goods they carried from England and paid him too little for the tobacco they carried back from the colony. "What happened?" he asked, with a tone barely masking the indifference he felt toward the answer.

"We lost a yardarm and our rigging when lightning hit the mast, and two men when a wave washed over the deck. For a time, I didn't think we'd see Maryland again."

"I trust you didn't lose my cargo," said Taney, whose steely eyes suddenly were fixed on Darby. "My warehouse is almost empty. I've orders for all the cloth and tools you've brought me."

Darby caught the threat in Taney's words and paused before replying.

"I have your cargo. You know you can count on me, Mister Taney."

"What about that carpenter you promised? I need a skilled man to build more barns for curing tobacco and a cooperage to produce hogsheads to ship the weed."

"Your carpenter was lost to the sea. He was helping my man clear the rigging from the deck when a wave washed them overboard. I lost two good men to that devilish storm."

"So you've no new men to indenture into my service?"

"No men, but here are the carpenter's children, Paul and Rebecca, ready to work."

"What?" cried Taney, anger rising in his hard-edged voice. "You expect me to take these ragged, scrawny children? Don't play me for the fool, captain. Others have tried and paid dearly for that error."

"That was our arrangement, a carpenter and his family," Darby replied, determined not to back down in the face of Taney's anger.

"Why, that boy's just skin and bones," replied Taney. "He's too young to grow whiskers. His tiny sister is thin as a willow whip. She wouldn't last a month working the tobacco. What good is she to me?"

"What about the twenty pounds sterling you agreed to pay for their passage?"

"I'll take the cloth and tools, but not these wretched children."

"What should I do with them?"

"For all I care," said Taney in disgust, "cut them up and use them as bait to catch fish in the Bay. They're no use to me.

"But what about that young fellow with the shackles and chains on his wrists?" asked Taney. "He looks strong enough to survive the seasoning."

"McNeely? He's for sale."

"Good! I need more men to work my fields."

"I warn you," said Darby. "He's a rough one. He had a bad reputation in London, but I agreed to carry him here to Maryland by request of the authorities."

"What's he done?"

"On the crossing, my mate found him threatening this girl. He was stealing the children's food. We searched his possessions and found other things stolen from the crew. We put him in irons and kept him locked below decks for the rest of the voyage."

"I'll pay a fair passage price for him and take his indenture for five years."

"He's yours for twelve pounds sterling, but don't hold me responsible for his conduct."

Taney cast a harsh glance at McNeely and then at Darby. Was this captain questioning his judgment?

"I've an overseer who knows how to handle his type. A season of clearing fields for tobacco will take the fight out of him. Prepare his contract and I'll pay your price."

"I'll send my men down to the wharf to get the cloth and tools as soon as you bring the goods from the *Providence*. You'll get full payment for those things too."

With that, Taney turned abruptly and walked away without another word to the captain or the two men who'd been standing with him in front of the inn. Darby knew better than to argue with Taney. His power and wealth controlled Battle Town. But what should he do with Rebecca and Paul?

A tall, broad-shouldered young man who had been standing near Taney stepped forward. "What's the boy's price? I need a young lad to help my wife with her vegetables and corn."

Captain Darby turned to the new speaker in surprise. He was young, with long, black hair tied with a simple string behind his head. Unlike Taney, he wore the plain clothes of men who worked the tobacco fields for planters around the Bay.

"And who are you sir?" asked Darby, passing his keen eye over the stranger to take a measure of the man. "I may sell you the boy if you are of good character and meet my price. But I owe it to his father to know something about the man who buys him."

"I'm Matthew DaSilva," answered the young man, whose broad shoulders, powerful arms and deeply tanned face were so different from Taney.

"I'm a boat builder and have 250 acres of land and four men who work my fields. I'm not wealthy like Taney, but I'll make a fair deal with you."

"I'll take ten pounds sterling for the boy," replied Darby, wondering if his price would be out of reach of this stranger and leave him with no buyer for Paul or Rebecca.

Paul felt Rebecca's hand tighten and begin to shake at the captain's words. Don't start crying now, thought Paul. He pulled his sister closer to his side, as if his arm around her would comfort and protect her.

"The price is fair," said DaSilva with a smile, enjoying the work of buying and selling and the negotiations that always were necessary in every sale.

"I don't have the ten pounds sterling you require. Taney may be able to pay you with true English coins, but few others have that type of wealth here in Maryland. If you're willing to enter into trade with me, here's what I'll offer in return. I'll repair the rigging on your ship and any other damage done by the storm."

Darby looked directly into Matthew's eyes. Is this stranger trying to take advantage of me? Does he know my ship will barely sail without the repairs? Is he someone I can trust? "I need those repairs," said Darby, deciding to test the young stranger further. "But they're not worth ten pounds sterling. I'll not sell this young boy for less than my full price."

"Then for the remainder, I'll bring you 1,000 board feet of lumber each spring for four years," replied Matthew. "You can use the lumber to repair your vessel or carry it back to London where it'll fetch a good price."

This young man knows the value of his work and the lumber he's offering, thought Darby. He has more experience than I'd expect to find in someone his age. "I'll accept your payments," said Darby, extending his hand to end the bargaining. "But only with a written contract to protect my interests."

"Done," said DaSilva, pleased to gain another worker for his household. "Prepare the contract and I'll sign it today."

"And I'll purchase the girl," said Thomas Cosgrove, "now that I see you're accepting barter."

Darby looked at the innkeeper in surprise. "Why do you need a girl this young?"

"Governor Calvert appointed me a county judge for Battle Town. When court's in session, the inn is so busy I need the extra help."

"What's your offer?"

"I'll provide pork and cider for five years for your trips to England. I'll cure the pork in salt so it doesn't spoil on your journey home and pack it in oak casks you can store with your cargo. My cider is known as the best on this side of the Bay. It's more than a fair price for a girl so young, slender, and weak. Do you accept?"

"Your offer's as fair as the boat builder's. I'll sell you Rebecca for five years, and he can take Paul."

The Punch will be a safe home for Rebecca, thought Darby. She wouldn't last a season working in the tobacco fields. And now I can get on with my business without the burden of these children.

"I'll draw up the contracts, gentlemen. Let's meet in the inn this evening to sign them over a tankard of your good cider, Master Cosgrove. "

"That's settled then," said DaSilva, who turned quickly to Paul. "Come along, boy. I can't get the repairs done to the *Providence* standing in front of the Punch."

Paul hesitated, not knowing what to do. Things are happening so fast, he thought. What does it mean that I'm sold to this boat builder? How can I protect Rebecca if she belongs to the innkeeper? What has Captain Darby done to us?

"Leave your sister and your clothing here, boy," said DaSilva, with a hint of impatience in his voice. "We'll return when the work's finished."

Paul could see fear in Rebecca's face. He could see the tears gathering in her eyes. "It'll be alright," he said, releasing Rebecca's hand. "We'll be here together."

"But Paul," cried his sister, who grabbed hold of his arm with both hands.

"You stay here," said Paul firmly, pulling himself free from her grasp.

"I'll see you when I return from the *Providence*." Rebecca started to cry.

"Go with the innkeeper and take our clothes with you. Battle Town is our new home. You'll be safe here."

Without another word, Paul turned and hurried after his new master, who was striding back down the hill toward the wharf. She'll be alright, thought Paul. We both have new masters and work and a place to live. I know I can protect her here. If only she'd stop crying.

2

Aboard the Providence

Paul sat quietly in Matthew's log canoe as the big man rowed out to the *Providence*. Matthew hadn't spoken to Paul since they left Rebecca behind at the Punch. Paul wanted to ask his new master many questions. But he sensed he should be quiet and only speak when Matthew spoke to him. So he tried to forget the doubts and questions running through his mind.

The canoe moved rapidly through the water, traveling faster than Captain Darby's skiff even though two sailors had been at the oars and Matthew rowed alone. Matthew's oars made no sound when they entered the water. The canoe silently picked up speed with each stroke.

Again I'm on the water, thought Paul. Again it's back to the *Providence*, the ship that killed my father. Will I never escape a life of ships and the sea?

When they reached the *Providence*, Paul caught hold of the rope ladder and quickly climbed up to the deck. Matthew tied the canoe to the bottom of the ladder, and then followed. They were alone. All of the crew had gone ashore, eager to eat and drink at the Punch after many weeks at sea.

Matthew walked around the shattered deck and the gaping hole where the yardarm and rigging had crashed down during the storm. First he paced the length. Then he paced the width.

"It'll take nearly thirty square feet of oak to repair this damage," Matthew said, almost to himself. "I'd do it in a day back at my boatyard where I've the lumber and tools. But with only an axe and a mallet in the canoe, it could take three days just to repair this decking. And that assumes I'll find the proper oak somewhere on shore."

Paul watched his new master pacing around the damaged deck, wondering what to do. Should he wait for orders from Matthew? Should he tell him what he knew? Finally, he decided to speak. "Sir," said Paul, "the ship's carpenter kept an adze, his hatchets, awls, chisels, and planes in his locker below, and there's a large store of lumber and timbers close by. Will that help you with the repairs?"

"How do you know the tools I'll need? What do you know of lumber?"

Matthew's voice sounded harsh. Paul hesitated before answering, wondering if he had angered his new master.

"Well sir," Paul said, trying to keep the fear out of his voice, "my father was a carpenter in Bristol. For the last three years I worked with him each day. I'd go and get the tools or things he needed. Over the last year he taught me to use the awls, chisels, and planes. During the voyage, the ship's carpenter let me help him make small repairs."

"Well then, boy, what are you waiting for? Show me these tools. There's work to be done. If the supplies are as ample as you suggest, we'll repair this deck by sundown."

It was noon before Matthew had cut away all of the broken sections of the deck. While he removed the damaged lumber, Paul carried the replacement oak up from the hold and assembled the tools needed to complete the repairs. The hours had passed with almost no words between them. Paul could feel questions building up in his mind. But he dared not speak or risk angering this man who now owned him.

For the second time that day, Paul's thoughts drifted back to his father. Working with his father had been the happiest time in his life. Now, working with Matthew, he felt empty.

Matthew hardly spoke. When he did, he used a sharp, commanding voice that left Paul afraid. This man is not like my father, thought Paul. I must watch him carefully. What will he do if I make a mistake? Feelings of loss and fear flooded his mind.

Matthew had just set down his hatchet and was surveying the morning's work when Captain Darby climbed up the ladder. "You're making good progress."

"That we are," replied Matthew. "At first I thought the work would take days. But this boy is proving more useful than I expected. He may be worth more in my boatyard than growing food with my wife."

"Speaking of food," said Darby, "I've brought an oyster pie and a cask of cider from the Punch. Cosgrove's cook does a much better job than our cook here on the *Providence*. If you stay on board this evening, you'll sample his food. So enjoy something more tasty now."

Matthew's words about his work surprised Paul. Matthew had said almost nothing to him throughout the morning. As he sat down to eat, Paul decided to risk a question. "Please, sir, am I to be your apprentice or your indentured servant?"

Matthew didn't answer. As the minutes passed and the silence grew, Paul began to fear he'd made a mistake. So he returned to his food. Matthew, too, continued to eat. Finally he set aside his meal, took a drink of the cider, and turned toward Paul.

"I'm paying your passage. That makes you my servant. You'll do as I say for the next five years. I'm your master."

"Yes, sir."

"For your labors, I'll provide food, some clothes, and a place to sleep. That's the life of an indentured servant here in Maryland."

"Yes, sir."

"My father, Jose DaSilva, came to Maryland with the first settlers that Lord Baltimore sent from England on the Ark and the Dove. He too was an indentured servant, bound to work for the Jesuit Fathers who paid for his passage."

"What happened to him, sir?"

"For five years he served Father White as his boatman, rowing the good Father up the Potomac and around the Bay as he worked to convert the native peoples to Catholicism."

"And then, sir?"

"He earned his freedom."

"What will happen…to me?"

"You'll serve me for five years. It'll be your good fortune if you survive and learn something about building boats. But I promise you no more than food, some clothes, and a place to sleep. For five years you'll do as I say. I'm your master."

"Does that mean, sir, I must become a Catholic?"

"No. Lord Baltimore's laws forbid forced conversion to any religion."

"I was baptized an Anglican."

"The colony's Assembly enacted laws of tolerance that allow all

Christian faiths to practice in Maryland. That is the policy of the Calverts and the law in their colony."

"And you, sir?"

"I'm a Catholic, as was my father. Your faith is your own choice and not part of your indenture. Enough talk. We've work to do before the sun sets."

Paul didn't want the conversation to end. He'd many more questions. Where would he sleep? What about Rebecca? What would he do after five years? But he held back and set his questions and doubts aside. Silence was the best choice. Clearly, Matthew didn't like idle talk. The afternoon went quickly. Matthew measured and cut the oak planks to fit into sections of deck he'd removed. When each board was properly shaped, Paul drilled holes with an awl on the planks that Matthew had marked. Then Matthew would set the plank back and drive wooden pegs into each hole to secure it to the wooden beams that supported the deck.

When the last plank was in place, Matthew stepped back to survey the work. "It's a good repair, solid and complete. Tomorrow we'll shape a timber into the new yardarm for the mast. Then we can go home to South River.

Home to South River, thought Paul? What did that mean? He felt puzzled. They were in Battle Town along Battle Creek. What does Matthew mean they'll go home to South River?"

Before Paul could ask, Matthew climbed back down the rope ladder and into his canoe. Paul followed. His mind raced with questions. But he sat in silence. Finally, as they neared the wharf, he asked, "What do you mean, sir, that we'll go home to South River? I thought your home was here in Battle Town or at least close by on Battle Creek."

"No one said you'd remain here in Battle Town."

"Where's South River?"

"It's a day's sail to the north. I live there with my wife, child, and mother. In two days we'll sail to my home. You'll not return here to Battle Creek until next year."

"What will happen to Rebecca?"

"Your sister's not my concern. She's indentured to Cosgrove and must work for him. You'll see her again when we return next year."

Matthew's words sat like a stone on Paul's heart. Next year! How could he leave Rebecca behind? How could he tell her they'd not be together? Paul felt the heavy weight of his questions. Sadness nearly overwhelmed him.

3

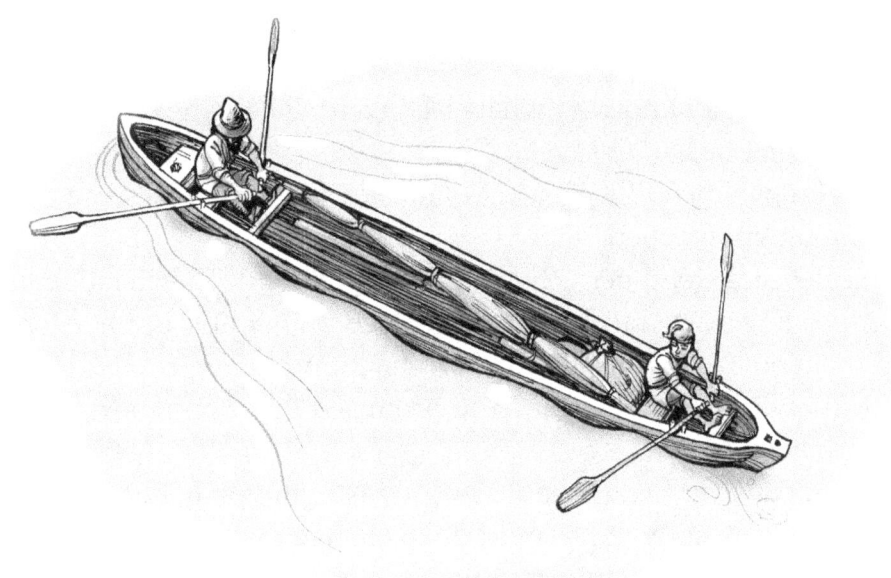

Sailing to South River

Early on the third day, Paul silently followed Matthew back down to the wharf. The air was cold. A light fog sat on the water like a soft, gray blanket. The sun was barely visible above the tall oaks on the other side of Battle Creek, where the *Providence* sat quietly at anchor.

Paul had been dreading this day. He'd hardly spoken to Matthew or Rebecca all morning. His mind had been racing. How to tell Rebecca he was going away? How to tell her he was leaving her behind?

Paul thought back to the first night when they returned after repairing the *Providence*. Rebecca had been busy serving food and cleaning up after customers. She moved quickly about the inn from table to table. She hardly had time to stop and sit with Paul and Matthew when she served them their food. That had been fine with Paul.

Paul had noticed that evening that Rebecca's eyes were red because she'd been crying again. But he said nothing. How could he tell her he'd be leaving her behind when Matthew took him away to South River?

Finally, on this third morning, when Rebecca brought their food and drink, he knew he had to tell her.

"Rebecca," he said in a low, quivering voice, "my master and I are leaving Battle Town today. He's taking me away to his home, which is in some place called South River. And he's said that you have to stay here as a servant to Mr. Cosgrove."

Paul hesitated, not knowing what else to add. Finally he blurted out the worst part of what he had to say.

"I don't know when I'll be back. My master says it will be some time next year. But I don't know when."

At first Rebecca stood perfectly still, staring at Paul. Then a look of fear came over her. She started to cry. Words formed on her lips. But her sobs drowned them out. After several minutes she found her voice.

"Paul…how can you leave me? You promised this would be our home. Why did you lie to me?"

Paul didn't answer her. He could feel her fear and pain. But he was going away, and there was nothing he could do to change that.

Rebecca just stared at Paul. Her thin body hardly moved, except for the spasms of sobs rising up from her waist and ending in her throat.

Finally Matthew stood up from the table and spoke. "Quiet yourself, girl. You are to stay here and work for your master. Now go away and do that. Paul's my servant. He'll return in twelve months and see you then. Paul," Matthew said, locking his eyes on the boy, "it's time to go."

Paul silently rose from the bench, turned away from his sister, and without a word followed his master out of the inn. His feet felt like stones as he slowly walked behind Matthew down the path to Battle Creek.

When they reached the wharf and canoe, Matthew climbed in first. He lifted a wide, flat board with a long handle and placed it into the water at the back of the canoe. Then he carefully moved toward the front of the craft, placing his feet with care to keep the narrow canoe from tipping over. When he reached the bow, he lifted the tall mast that lay in the bottom of the canoe and placed it into a slot carved into the solid front of the craft. Matthew attached the sail to the mast and tied a rope to the top of the sail to hoist it up the mast. When he finished, he turned to Paul.

"You'll row us out into the harbor so I can set our sail as soon as we're clear of the wharf. Now push off and steer out into Battle Creek. Keep the bow pointed directly into the wind. You'll know you're on course when you feel the wind at the back of your head. If you feel it on your cheek, pull harder on the opposite side of the canoe to bring the bow back into the wind."

Paul used one of the oars to push the canoe away from the wharf. Then he placed the oars in between the wooden pins set into the gunnels on each side of the canoe, just as he'd seen Matthew set the oars over the past two days. He dipped the ends of the oars into the water and pulled. The canoe hardly moved.

"Push your hands forward with the oars out of the water," instructed Matthew. "Then raise your hands until the oars drop into the water and pull with all of your strength. When your hands hit your chest, drop them down and move them all the way forward again with the oars out of the water."

Paul tried to follow Matthew's directions. At first he couldn't keep his two hands moving at the same rate. The front of the canoe started to turn in a circle to the right. The next time, it moved back toward the left. Paul kept rowing, expecting to hear Matthew's voice venting his frustration at his incompetent servant. But he only heard the water striking against the sides of the canoe.

Paul kept rowing, despite the tension rising up his back and arms. Finally the canoe seemed to be moving forward. Paul concentrated on keeping the wind at his back.

"Keep her steady now," said Matthew calmly. "You're doing fine. I'm going to raise the sail. Once it's up, stop rowing and pull in the oars. I'll come back and join you and take the rudder to keep us on course."

A minute later, Matthew was sitting next to Paul. He held a rope tied to the end of the sail in one hand and the long arm of the rudder in the other. As the wind filled the sail, the canoe began to gain speed. Soon it was moving faster than even Matthew could row.

"You handled the canoe well, boy. Now settle yourself in the bow. We have a long day of sailing before us. But with a fair breeze, we'll reach South River before day's end."

The wharf and Battle Town moved away behind them. They passed the *Providence* and headed quickly down toward the mouth of Battle Creek and out into the broad, deep blue waters of the Patuxent River. Paul was glad to put this ship of sadness behind him with its cargo of harsh memories.

The rising sun began to warm him as it burned the fog off the top of the water. But it didn't warm his heart. Perhaps all the pain is not on that ship, he thought, as his mind reached back toward his little sister, now alone in the inn in Battle Town.

Sailing in the canoe was different than sailing across the Atlantic on the *Providence*. Even when the winds were strong, the big ship barely seemed to move through the water. In the canoe, Paul could reach down and touch the water as it raced past the side. Each shift in the wind tilted the canoe to one side or another. Soon Paul was feeling the excitement of sailing. He watched in amazement as Matthew constantly made small adjustments with the rudder and the angle of the sail to keep the canoe moving. This man was a master of his craft.

When he was aboard the *Providence*, Paul could not wait to leave the ship. Now, for the first time, Paul felt real joy out on the water. He wanted to learn to sail. But for today he was happy to feel the sun on his face and to leave the work in Matthew's strong, steady hands.

As they sailed down the Patuxent, Paul's mind wandered. Sometimes he'd think about Rebecca, and feelings of helpless came over him. Then something along the river would catch his eye and the excitement would return. There was so much to see, so much to learn.

He caught sight of a clearing along one of the river's banks where several log canoes were pulled up on the sand. Further down they passed a ship about the size of the *Providence* anchored at the mouth of another river that ran into the Patuxent.

"That's St. Leonard's Creek," said Matthew. "There are as many plantations up that water as you will find on Battle Creek. I've sold eight log canoes to plantation owners there and expect to sell more in the coming years. Some of the ship captains prefer to stay anchored here in the Patuxent and have the plantation owners bring their hogsheads of tobacco to them in their canoes. That creates many buyers for my canoes all along this mighty river."

What's this, thought Paul? Matthew has said more to me since we left the wharf than he has in the past two days. He seems different somehow, out here on the water.

Further down the river, Paul noticed the banks on either side were moving away from their canoe. As his eye followed one bank, he saw the great trees that lined the sides of the river begin to disappear. Suddenly open water lay before them. They were reaching the end of the Patuxent and about to enter the great waters of Chesapeake Bay that stretched far out ahead of them.

Matthew sailed directly into the Bay. Paul wondered if Matthew planned to sail back to the Atlantic Ocean. He was about to ask when Matthew said, "Watch your head now. I'm about to turn north. When I move the rudder, this sail will get blown across the canoe. If you're not careful, the pole at the bottom of the sail will strike you as it comes across."

With that Matthew pulled the long rudder handle to the other side of the canoe and the bow cut a graceful curve through the waters to the left. The sail seemed to stand still for a moment. Then as the wind caught its outside edge, the pole swung quickly across the canoe.

Now they were headed back toward the shoreline. Here the land rose sharply from the water's edge, climbing thirty or forty feet almost straight up. More tall trees crowded up to the edge of the cliff, forming a wooden wall the eye could not penetrate.

Water birds flocked along the shoreline. Larger birds circled high overhead. "The larger birds are eagles," said Matthew. "They rule the shoreline up and down the Bay. The smaller birds we call fish hawks. If you watch carefully, you'll see them dive straight down, plunge into the water, and come back up with a fish in their beaks. The eagles will fly across the top of the water and pull out even larger fish with their sharp claws."

Please keep talking, thought Paul. There is so much to learn. There is so much to see. I have so many questions.

"This Bay feeds all of the people who've come to its shores," said Matthew.

"This Bay can feed all the eagles, fish hawks, and waterfowl that fly over its waters. The forests provide deer and bears and turkeys for our guns. We can grow enough corn and vegetables in a good year to last through the winter. If a man's prepared to work hard, he can grow enough tobacco to purchase everything he needs from the ships that come from England."

"But this Bay also has its dangers, just like the sea. Don't be mistaken by this fine day out on these waters. This Bay provides for us, but can take from us too."

"Five years ago I sailed with my father to the top of the Bay. Jose had a license from Lord Baltimore for the beaver trade. He'd purchase beaver skins from the Susquahannock people who ruled the forests in the north of the Bay. Then he'd sell them to the ship captains in St. Mary's City."

"We'd filled half of one of the canoes with beaver from the river they call the Patapsco, and then sailed to the mouth of the Susquahanna River where he purchased most of his skins. When my canoe was full, he sent me back to our home on South River. He was going to wait two more days to see if the Susquahannocks who lived further north would bring down more skins to fill his canoe."

"Two days after I arrived home the worst storm in my lifetime roared up the Bay. It destroyed all of the tobacco and corn plants growing in the fields on both sides of the Chesapeake. Trees fell. Houses were torn apart. There was destruction everywhere. We waited for Jose. He didn't return.

"After the storm passed, I sailed back out to the Bay to search for him. As I crossed the mouth of the Severn River, which lies just north of our home, I saw Jose's log canoe washed far up on the shore. The mast was broken. There were no oars or beaver pelts. There was no sign of Jose.

"There's much beauty to this Bay. And the land can be generous. But never forget that death is always close at hand."

Matthew's words surprised Paul. Was it a warning or a prophecy?

On this warm spring day, Paul didn't want to accept Matthew's words. He didn't want to believe more hardships lay ahead.

Matthew has survived, thought Paul. I will too. I'll watch him and learn from him. I'll learn to sail. I'll get back to Battle Town to watch over Rebecca. I'll earn my freedom.

4

The Switch

Rebecca awoke in the cold, dark shed where Mama Ailsworth prepared food for the inn. Her body was tired. She wanted to rest, to stay on her straw mattress, even through her thin blanket hardly kept her warm. But she was afraid. Her master would be angry. Her body begged for sleep, but she knew it was time to work.

Wrapping her blanket around her shoulders, Rebecca picked up the two wooden pails that stood by the door and walked out into the cold, early morning air to fetch water from the inn's springhouse. These first few days had been a nightmare. Her work began before dawn. She'd fetch water and fill the large cooking kettle, return for more water, bring in the firewood, and start the fire in the large hearth where Mama Ailsworth would spend her day cooking. Pleasing Mama was important. She was the only person in the inn who showed Rebecca any kindness.

As soon as Mama arrived, Rebecca helped her prepare the morning meals for the inn's guests, the innkeeper, and his family. There was corn to grind into a fine powder in the large wooden mortar and pestle that stood in one corner. Then Rebecca had to run out to the smokehouse where the innkeeper kept the large casks of salted pork. She'd cut out enough for Mama to fry up for breakfast. Then she'd rush back to the cooking shed and gather the plates, utensils, and bowls for serving the food.

Every few minutes, Rebecca would run between the cooking shed and the main room of the inn to see if any guests had come in for their meals. As soon as the first person entered the room, Rebecca had to start serving the food. She'd spend the next two hours bringing food from the cooking shed and clearing away the utensils, bowls, plates, and drinking cups after the guests were done.

When all the food was served, Rebecca would pick up any scraps of food that had dropped under the tables. After the last guest departed, she'd sweep out the entire room so that it was clean and ready for the next meal.

If neither the innkeeper nor Mrs. Cosgrove were in the room, Rebecca might take a few minutes to eat the porridge and ham Mama saved for her in the cooking shed. But if either of them remained, Rebecca had to clean the entire room before eating her first meal of the day. She was afraid to stop. She knew how easy it was to anger her master, and was afraid of what he'd do.

After the main room was clean, Rebecca would return to the cooking shed to clean the bowls, plates, and cups from the morning meal. First she'd scrape any remaining food from the plates and bowls into a special bucket that stood by the hearth. Next she'd carry the dirty dishes and cups out into the yard, and wash them in a bucket of cold water. After returning everything to the shelves on the shed wall, Rebecca would carry the bucket with the leftover food out to the pens where the innkeeper kept the pigs he was raising for this fall's slaughter. And that was just the morning's work.

Rebecca's afternoon and evening continued in the same way. She helped prepare the food, served the meals, swept out the main room, cleaned up the dishes, and cleaned out the cooking shed. She kept moving all day, with no time to rest.

The only good time was when Rebecca could stand near the hearth and help Mama prepare the meals. Mama had a gentle way about her. Often she'd be singing in a low voice as she worked at the hearth. From time to time she'd stop to show Rebecca how to slice strips of pork, or cut up squash for a stew, or cut open oysters and other shellfish when she was preparing one of her special dishes. It always was: "Rebecca, dear, bring me this, or do that, or help me here." She never yelled or got upset. She always set something good aside for Rebecca to eat. Rebecca had never lived or worked with a person like Mama Ailsworth. The woman's dark, radiant skin, the musical quality of her speech and the tightly curled hair on her head had seemed strange to Rebecca the first day in the shed. Now Rebecca wanted to be with Mama all the time. Mama was Rebecca's refuge for the few hours they shared together each day.

But those few hours disappeared faster than the food Rebecca carried out to the pigs. She spent most of her time running back and forth between the main room and the cooking shed, carrying food to the guests, and bringing the dirty dishes back to the shed, morning, noon and night. And then she had to clean.

Even after everything was clean and Mama had left the shed for the day, Rebecca's work continued. She was responsible for serving guests the hard cider and beer the innkeeper sold to travelers and local townspeople each evening. Some nights the drinking and talking could last nearly to midnight. Only then, after everything was cleared out of the main room, the room cleaned, and the drinks and cups stored away, could Rebecca return to the shed to sleep.

After her first day of work, Rebecca had fallen exhausted to her bed. Every muscle in her young body had ached. She could not keep her eyes open. She'd felt empty inside.

The second night in the inn, Rebecca had cried herself to sleep when she realized that every day for the next five years would look the same. How could it become worse?

Thomas Cosgrove answered that question the third night.

Rebecca felt exhaustion creeping up on her that third day. Her brother and his master had left her behind. Her body was weak from the constant work. She had to push herself to clean the main room after the noon meal. When she returned to the cooking shed to help Mama, Rebecca wanted to fall down and sleep on her straw mattress in the corner. But she knew Mama needed her help. The inn was full. They'd have to prepare more food than usual for that night's meal.

When Rebecca served the Cosgrove family and guests that evening, she could barely move one foot in front of the other. After she'd served the first two tables, guests in the inn began to complain about waiting for their food, or that the food was cold by the time Rebecca brought it to their table.

Rebecca tried to move faster. She began carrying three and four plates at a time. As soon as she placed the food in front of the guests, she turned quickly to get out of the room and back to the shed for more. Some of the quests continued to complain.

Rebecca was moving across the main room toward the shed when she saw the innkeeper standing by the door. He looked at her with a cold stare. "Move faster, you lazy girl," he shouted across the room. Rebecca kept walking toward the door.

As she passed through the door, Rebecca felt a sharp pain shoot across the back of her legs. Cosgrove had hit her with a willow switch he was holding in his hand. Rebecca cried out in surprise, pain, and fear. Cosgrove hit her again.

"You'll get more of the same if you keep my guests waiting for their food!"

Rebecca ran to the shed. That night she cried herself to sleep. But sleep did not come easily. Questions filled her mind. Is this my life? Paul, why have you abandoned me?

Rebecca cried for her brother. She cried for her dead father. She cried for herself until sleep closed over her. She even cried in her dreams.

5

The Seasoning

Paul lay quietly on his straw mattress in the large room where Matthew's mother cooked for the family each day. The sun was not yet up. Everything was silent. No one else was awake. That was good. It was time to begin his day.

Each morning, Paul had to bring in wood, start the fire, and carry water back from the spring before Matthew, his wife Susan, daughter Martha, and mother Mary came down from their sleeping rooms on the second floor of the cabin. Paul enjoyed being alone for these chores. It gave him time to think about everything that had happened since he arrived in Maryland.

After three weeks on South River, Paul was getting accustomed to life with Matthew and his family. Mary was a wonderful cook. There was always enough to eat. Susan seldom spoke, but always smiled when Paul talked with her daughter, little Martha.

The hardest part was working all day in the gardens and the cornfields. Paul had to do the digging and hoeing for Mary and Susan to prepare the ground for the spring planting. The ground was still hard from the long frozen days of winter. Breaking the soil into fine pieces of dirt so that Mary and Susan could plant their seeds took all of his strength.

After the first two days, Paul's hands had become raw with blisters. His arms and back ached. At night he'd fall asleep as soon as he finished the evening stew of corn and salt pork. In the morning his body hurt. The pain didn't go away until he was back working in the fields. It was good to concentrate on shaping the mounds of dirt where Mary and Susan would plant corn, beans, and squash. As the mounds began to stretch across the fields, he'd slowly forget the pain in his hands, his arms, and his back.

But now the hardest digging was done for this season. Paul could feel that his arms and shoulders had become much stronger. At night he didn't fall asleep right away. He was even starting to enjoy playing with three-year-old Martha before Susan would carry her up to their sleeping room on the cabin's second floor.

When he first arrived on South River, Paul was surprised by Matthew's home. It was a large cabin, built out of solid logs rather than the board and beam construction others used in the colony. Paul thought it looked more like a fort than a house. Heavy oak planks formed the thick front door and shutters that could be used to cover the windows on the first floor. The second floor windows were more like narrow slits cut into the logs. When he asked about its unusual form, Matthew explained that his father had copied this construction from some Swedish settlers he'd met at the top of the Bay where they traded with the Susquahannocks for beaver skins. "It was good protection from attack," Matthew explained, "and Jose wanted to make sure his family would be safe here on South River."

Paul had wondered why Jose needed to protect his family from attack. But he didn't ask. He knew Matthew didn't like to be questioned.

Still enjoying the quiet of the morning, Paul rose from his sleeping mattress and got to work starting the day's fire. As soon as the logs were burning, he left the cabin to gather more wood and water for cooking. When he came back, Mary was at the fireplace preparing the day's first meal. She did most of the cooking, leaving Susan to take care of Martha.

Matthew was sitting at the family table. Paul marveled at how much Matthew and his mother looked alike. Matthew had Mary's straight black hair, dark complexion, high cheekbones, and angular face. Of course he was much larger in his arms and shoulders. But like his mother, he was tall and lean. Both moved quickly in everything they did. And like her son, Mary worked hard all day, speaking only when necessary.

"Paul," said Matthew, "there'll be no work for you in the fields today. As soon as you finish your morning meal, meet me at the log canoes. We'll be sailing to my lands on the Severn River. It's time to gather this year's rents from my tenants and replenish the supply of logs and lumber for this season's work in the boatyard."

Sailing, thought Paul. He'd forgotten the wonderful feeling of being out on the Bay during all of the hard days in the cornfields. As he rushed to finish his food and race down to the river's edge, he felt excited about being on the water again.

But Paul was disappointed with the sail to the Severn. The journey took much less time than their sail from Battle Creek. The morning sun was not half way toward noon when Matthew brought the canoe on to a clearing on the north side of the Severn.

"This is the first land my father purchased from Lord Baltimore after he secured his freedom from indenture. The area was part of the Susquehannock hunting grounds. Most colonists feared coming here. But Jose knew that as long as he respected the rights of the Susquehannock hunters, he and his family would be safe. Here he'd have his home half way between St. Mary's City and the northern reaches of the Bay where he gathered his furs. He brought Mary here as his bride and I was born on this land one year later."

"But I thought he built his home on South River?"

"That was his second home. When the Puritans who settled here by the grace of Lord Baltimore took up arms in rebellion against the governor and the Lord Proprietor, my father remained loyal to the Calverts and stood against the Puritans. His Puritan neighbors never forgave him. After defeating Lord Baltimore's forces, they called him a Catholic traitor and threatened to burn his home."

"So he decided to move his family to land on South River that he purchased from Captain William Burdett who had settled that area and was loyal to the Calverts. Jose had been selling beaver pelts to Captain Burdett for several years, and Burdett welcomed him. But to be safe, Jose built his new home like that of the Swedish traders who lived among the Susquahannock people at the top of the Bay."

"Who lives here now?"

"My father was a fur trader. He didn't have time for farming or have any interest in raising tobacco. After he acquired the land from Lord Baltimore, he purchased two indentured servants with monies from the beaver trade. He built a second home for these two men. They cleared the land for corn and tobacco. My mother taught them how to grow beans and squash among the corn plants. Life for them and us was good until the Puritans drove us away."

"By that time, each man had only one year left on his contract to my father. Since they were not Catholics and were not hated by the Puritans, they agreed to stay on the land as my father's tenants after their final year of indenture. Now they raise their own tobacco, corn, and other food and pay me a yearly rent in return. Each pays me one hogshead of tobacco. Together they cut white pine and oak for me during the winter to pay the remainder of their rent. In this way I'm able to use the tobacco I get as rent to pay my yearly taxes and fees to the Calverts, and I get half the logs and lumber I'll use in my boatyard."

"That's why we're here. Today we're going to build a raft out of the three white pine logs and oak planks that are in the clearing. Tomorrow you'll go with me into the forest. We'll cut the bark around the base of each white pine and oak tree my tenants will harvest next winter.

"Now let's get to work. We'll start by rolling these three logs down into the water. Then we'll place the planks across the logs and secure them together with wooden pegs to form a raft. When the raft is solid, we'll pile the remaining planks on top so we can pull the entire load back to the boatyard. Go get the awl, the mallet, and wooden pegs from the canoe."

Paul wondered how he and Matthew would move the thirty-foot logs across the clearing and into the water. He guessed it would take ten men to lift one of them. He knew that Matthew was strong. But how could just the two of them move these logs?

Matthew surprised him when he placed a set of planks in a line on the ground running between the first log and the river. Then he placed a second row of planks parallel to the first row, but about fifteen feet apart.

Next, Matthew stacked eight planks on the opposite side of one of the logs.

"Now pick up one of the planks by your feet," said Matthew, "and do exactly as I do." Matthew inserted his plank under the log. Part of the plank rested on the stack of boards he had set behind it. Paul placed his plank in the same position and waited for Matthew's next order.

"Paul, pull down on the top end of your plank."

Matthew did the same. With both pulling down on their planks, the log began to move forward and started to roll across the planks toward the water. Half way to the river, it stopped.

This time, Paul knew what to do. He and Matthew moved the pile of planks down behind the log again. Then, with their planks in place, they pulled down on their levers and set the log moving toward the river. This time it rolled all the way to the water. Repeating these steps, they moved the other two logs down to the water's edge.

With the three logs floating in the water, it was easy to push them together, leaving one end facing the land and the other pointed out into the river. Matthew set the first plank across the three logs. "Use your awl to drill holes in the plank. Drill right down into each log. Then we'll set pegs into the holes and join the logs together."

Paul was amazed at how fast Matthew worked. As soon as he drilled a hole, Matthew pounded down a peg into the plank and log. By the time he had drilled two more holes, Matthew had tied the three logs together with the plank and set the second plank in place for Paul to drill. They kept at this pace until Paul had drilled thirty holes and Matthew had built a platform of planks across the three pine logs. Then, without stopping, Matthew started to carry the remaining oak planks on to their new raft. Paul had to race to keep up with him.

The sun was high above their heads when Paul reached down to pick up one of the last planks remaining on the ground. As he began to lift, his knee buckled. Suddenly he felt too weak to stand. Feeling hot and dizzy, he dropped to both knees.

Matthew moved up to Paul and placed his hand on Paul's forehead. "You have the fever. The seasoning has come on you!"

With that, he picked Paul up and carried him to the canoe. "I've got to get you back to Mary."

Paul didn't understand what had happened. He felt weak. He felt hot. All the strength had gone out of his body. He could barely think.

"What about the logs and lumber?" he asked weakly as he lay in the canoe.

"Don't concern yourself with the logs and timber," replied Matthew. "I can come back any time to pull this raft back to the South River. But if I don't get you back to Mary right away, you may die. You'll be no use to me dead from the seasoning."

6

The Recovery

Paul knew his mattress was close to the fire, but he still felt cold. His shirt was wet. He tried to sit up, but couldn't find the strength. His head fell back to the mattress. Someone had placed a thick blanket over him. He couldn't remember who, or when, or even how he came to be sleeping next to the fireplace. The last thing he remembered was lying in Matthew's canoe.

Paul shut his eyes. His head felt better with them closed. He was thirsty. The thought of trying to find some water made him feel exhausted again. Best to be quiet and just lay here, he thought. Perhaps I'm just dreaming. But how can I feel exhausted from a dream?

When Paul awoke again, Mary was kneeling next to him.

"Here," she said, "drink this." Paul put his lips to the bowl and took a deep drink. The liquid was bitter. He almost spit it back out on the floor, but stopped when he caught the look in Mary's eye.

"Drink all of it. You've been burning with fever for the past two days. We thought you were going to die of what these English call the seasoning."

Paul hesitated for a moment, not wanting to taste any more of the bitter drink. He now knew it was Mary who'd watched over him as he lay barely conscious for the past days and nights. "Thank you, Mary," he softly whispered as he finished the drink. "But why does my body still ache and feel so weak?"

"Your fever broke this morning. But you're still fighting the seasoning. This drink has kept you alive. So let it finish its work in your body. When you feel stronger I'll bring you something to eat."

"What am I drinking?"

"You don't have a name for it in your language. It is a drink my people, the Nanticoke, use when our children have the fever. It comes from the bark of the willow and the roots of the plant you call the sassafras. I learned it from my mother, who learned it from her mother."

"I don't understand," said Paul. "What do you mean, 'my people, the Nanticoke'?"

"I didn't come here like you, or like my husband, Jose, from the place you call England. Like my son, Matthew, I was born here on the Chesapeake. But that was on the other side of the Bay where my people fished and farmed and lived before any of your wooden ships sailed into these waters. That was long ago."

Paul still didn't understand. Was it the seasoning playing tricks with his mind? Was this Mary speaking, or some other person, or some dream voice caused by his sickness? "Then how did you come here? And why do you live here?"

"When I was younger than you are now," replied Mary, "Susquahannock warriors came to my village and took me away as a slave. I was raised among the Susquahannock on their great river to the north. It was there that Jose found me when he came to buy the skins of the beaver. He purchased me and took me to his home on the Severn to be his wife. But first we had to sail to St. Mary's City so that the Jesuit Fathers could make me a Catholic."

"Why did Jose force you to be a Catholic? Your son told me it's the law of this colony that no one can be forced to convert to any religion."

"Jose didn't force me. He explained I'd have no rights as his wife if I didn't accept a Christian faith. I might become a slave again if anything happened to him while I remained a Nanticoke. So I agreed to go with him to St. Mary's City and to accept the name of Mary which the Jesuit Fathers gave me when they baptized me."

"And what about your people, the Nanticoke? Do you ever go to see them? Or will they come to visit with us here on South River?"

"My people are gone. They've been driven from their lands by you English men who come here to grow tobacco and send it away in your ships.

"Even the mighty Susquehannock who sold beaver skins to Jose are gone from this land. First they fought with the English and their guns. Then the Seneca warriors came down from the north to destroy their villages on the

Susquehanna. And finally a great sickness came upon them and killed the young children and old people who'd been left behind by the warriors.

"Now Matthew and Susan and Martha are my family. By the time we've harvested the corn, Susan will add another child to this cabin. I am Mary. That is all. The Nanticoke are only a memory, like a dream. Rest now. You must sleep and regain your strength. When you wake I'll bring you some food and sweet cider to drink."

As Paul closed his eyes, he tried to imagine the people of Mary's story, the ones who were gone. They'd disappeared from this land, like Jose in the great storm. Matthew had said death was always near on the Chesapeake. Would he and Rebecca and all of the other English people disappear some day, like the Nanticoke and the Susquahannock?

7

The Promise

When Mama Ailsworth entered the cooking shed, she found Rebecca lying on her mattress. Strange, she thought. It wasn't like the young girl to neglect her duties.

"Becca," called out Mama, using her special name for the girl, "are you sick?" Only soft moans came back from across the room.

Crossing over to Rebecca, Mama bent down to feel the young girl's brow. Tears were running down Rebecca's face. Her hair was tangled. She was curled up on the mattress with her knees almost touching her head.

"Why are you crying, child?"

"The innkeeper's going to kill me. I heard him late last night when he was sitting in the main room drinking with a guest. It was dark. I don't think he saw me as I finished cleaning up the drinking cups and putting away the beer and cider."

"What do you mean, he's going to kill you?"

"The guest asked the innkeeper what he planned to do with me. The innkeeper said he was going to keep me for three years until I'd filled out like a good breeding sow. Then he'd sell me to a planter here on Battle Creek who'd know what to do with me."

Mama suppressed a smile as she listened to Rebecca. This poor, sweet child, she thought. She's an innocent in this world and doesn't know how men talk. But she didn't want to stop Rebecca from telling her tale. She knew the talking would help Rebecca get over her fear.

"Then what did the innkeeper say, Becca?"

"He said, 'Look at her now! If you cut her hair and put trousers on her, you couldn't tell whether she was a boy or a girl. I figure in three years her hips will widen and her breasts will swell. When she's good and plump in all the right places, I'll get twice what I paid to Captain Darby from some planter who wants to breed her.'"

Tears were streaming down Rebecca's face. Her voice dropped to a whisper.

"Does he plan to sell me for slaughter like those pigs I feed every day?"

"No Becca," said Mama, "that's not what he means. This man Cosgrove has a dark heart. But he doesn't plan to kill you or sell you to someone who will. Now get up and splash some water on your face. We've got to get busy preparing the morning meals. When that's done, I'll explain what the innkeeper means and what I'll do to make sure it doesn't happen."

Rebecca looked up at Mama. Slowly she got up from her mattress. She saw an iron-like determination in the big woman's face. Am I really safe, she thought. Can Mama protect me? She wasn't sure, but she knew her only hope was to do what Mama said and wait to learn what she meant.

Still feeling afraid, Rebecca walked to the door, picked up two buckets, and headed out to the springhouse. When she returned, Mama had started the fire in the hearth and was heading out the door to get more wood.

"You fill the kettle with those two buckets, Becca. Then go to the smokehouse and bring back two plates full of salt pork and the dozen eggs from the shelf. I'll grind the corn meal. We don't have much time before someone wants food. I'll whip up a batch of my special corn cakes. You can fry the pork. Keep the pork fat in the frying pan. When I have my corn meal ready, I'll fry my cakes in the fat. Those cakes will taste so sweet even the innkeeper won't mind if he has to wait for this morning's meal."

Rebecca and Mama worked in silence until the pork was cooked and Mama was frying her cakes. "Becca, you'd better check to see if anyone's in the main room. Take the cups and utensils with you. If Cosgrove and his family are there, just shout out that Mama Ailsworth is cooking up something special and didn't want you to bring in the food until someone was ready to eat."

Rebecca filled her arms with cups and utensils and headed to the main room. She was back in less than a minute. "Three guests are sitting at a table talking. The Cosgroves haven't come in yet. I told the guests that I'd be right back with their food. Is it ready?"

"I've these plates ready. Bring them to the guests and come back for more. In ten minutes I'll have enough done to set out plenty of cakes and ham for the guests and the innkeeper's family. When Cosgrove comes in, everything will be ready and waiting. That should keep him happy and out of our way for some time. Now go!"

Before she knew it, Rebecca had carried enough corn cakes and fried ham into the main room to feed twice the number of guests who'd stayed in the inn. When she got back to the shed, Mama handed her a plate of her own.

"Now let me explain what you heard last night," said Mama. "The innkeeper is planning to keep you until you grow into a young woman. Then he'll sell you to a planter who doesn't have a wife. That's his evil plan."

"But I don't want to be some planter's wife."

"I know. And as long as I am standing on these two feet, I won't let him."

A puzzled look came over Rebecca's face. "How can you stop him?"

"Let me tell you a thing or two about Mama Ailsworth," replied Mama. "I'm a free woman today, but I wasn't always free. At one time I was owned by Master Robert Brooke, who was the first man to settle in this area and whose son, Baker, is the largest and most powerful landowner in this place."

"Do you mean you were indentured, like me?"

"No, Becca, I wasn't indentured like you. I was owned as a slave. Master Brooke purchased me from a slave trader when I was about five years older than you. He was living in England, and had just gotten married to his first wife. He purchased me to be her house servant. As his slave, he owned me for my entire life. You only have to work for the innkeeper for five years. That's the difference between a slave and an indentured servant. You'll gain your freedom."

To Rebecca, Mama's words didn't make sense. Mama said she's free, but owned for life by Master Brooke. Rebecca was owned by Cosgrove, but would be free. How was that possible? She trusted Mama. She just didn't understand.

"Then how'd you become free?"

"When Mrs. Brooke was ready to give birth to her first child, who is the man we know as Baker Brooke today, she had a terrible time with the birth. She struggled for three days to birth that baby. When Baker was born, Mrs. Brooke was bleeding badly. Nothing I did, nothing the midwife tried to do, could stop the bleeding. I stayed by that woman's side for the next week, never leaving her room except when I went to get goat's milk for the baby. Mrs. Brooke was too weak to nurse that child. So I cared for her as much as I could, fed the baby, and watched over them both until she died.

"That's how I got the name Mama. I took care of that baby for the next three years. Even when Master Brooke came back to his estate with a new wife, I was the one who fed Baker and watched over him until he was big enough to take care of himself. It was Baker who started calling me Mama. His father started calling me Mama too. Then everyone in the family used that name for me.

"When Master Brooke decided to come to this place from England, he brought me along with all of his other servants, his wife, and eight children. I was the only slave. When Master Brooke died a few years later, Master Baker told me his father had instructed him in his will to give me my freedom. That's how I became free. And Baker purchased an acre of land for me here in Battle Town and had a small house built for me on that land.

"I was very happy being free. I had land to raise my own corn and vegetables, and all the herbs and spices I use in the cooking shed. I could get fish and oysters and clams and wild birds from the river. I even had enough left over to cook up special foods and pies and sell them here in Battle Town. That's why Cosgrove asked me to be his cook when he came here to open his inn.

"I told Cosgrove I was a free woman. I'd only work for him for fair payment and good treatment. That's why he never hit me. My food is the best part of his inn. I'll walk away if he mistreats me in any way."

"But how," asked Rebecca, "can you stop him from selling me to some planter?"

"As I said, Becca, this innkeeper has a dark heart and evil ways. But I know some of his secrets. I know some evil things he's done. If the innkeeper tries to sell you away from this place before you have your freedom, I'll tell him that I'll go to Master Baker Brooke and talk about his dark, evil secrets. Cosgrove won't be able to stay in Battle Town if his secrets are known. He'll not dare to sell you or harm you. So child, I may not be able to stop the innkeeper from hitting you with his switch. But I can keep you safe. And that's what I'll do.

"I'll make one more promise. By the time you leave this inn as a free woman, you'll be the second best cook in Battle Town. You'll be able to make your own way in this world just like I've done."

Rebecca looked at Mama in wonder. For the first time since Paul had left her, she felt safe. She wanted to tell Mama how good it felt, but the words didn't come.

"Now let's get back to work," said Mama. "They'll want their noon meal soon enough."

8

The Boatyard

After the fever broke, Paul slept for three days. Whenever he'd wake, Mary was there to give him food and drink. She was in charge of his care and recovery. So Paul just lay on his straw mattress, ate what he could, and waited for his strength to return.

At times he would watch little Martha play next to the wooden table where the family ate its meals. The rest of each day he lay quietly because Matthew was out at the boatyard and Susan was tending the corn and the garden with Martha at her side. Only Mary remained in the cabin to care for him, and she was as silent as her son and his wife.

On the fourth morning Paul felt well enough to start the fire and resume his chores. As he ate his bowl of corn meal, beans, and squash, Matthew asked, "Are you strong enough to join me in the boatyard?"

Mary gave Matthew a skeptical look, but said nothing.

Paul hesitated before answering. He knew he felt better. But was he strong enough to work in the boatyard? He didn't want to anger Matthew by appearing to be lazy, but wasn't sure he could work an entire day.

"Yes," he finally said, "I think I can work again."

Matthew nodded. A moment later he rose from the table and walked out of the cabin. Paul quickly swallowed the last bits of his morning meal and hurried to catch up with him.

When they reached the boatyard, Paul saw that Matthew had sailed again to the Severn and had brought the pine logs and oak planks back to the yard. The three logs were pulled up on the land, sitting parallel to each other. The planks were stacked in the shed where Matthew kept his tools and lumber.

"Paul, go get two hatchets, a saw, and my adze."

Paul went to the shed and returned with the tools.

"First we'll remove the bark from the log with hatchets. Watch how I do it on this side, and then go to the end and remove the bark on the other side."

Matthew started chopping the bark about four inches down from the top of the log. As usual, he worked quickly, making short, fast cuts every three or four inches down the side until he'd reached the curving, outer edge of the log. Then he stepped back along the tree's length and cut the next section of bark. Again he started cutting about four inches down from the top. As the axe split the bark away, he made a second, third and forth cut until he'd removed the bark right out to the log's outer edge. Moving back once more, Matthew repeated the process. After five minutes, the top quarter of the thirty-foot trunk was bare of bark for almost six feet of its length.

Paul watched Matthew for several minutes. Then he moved to the opposite side of the log to begin removing bark the same way. To his surprise, it was more difficult than Matthew made it appear. Paul's first cuts removed only small sections of bark. He looked at Matthew again. He noticed that Matthew cut down and on an angle, allowing the hatchet's edge to follow the curve of the wood. Paul tried again. With each stroke he cut off a larger section of bark.

As he began to feel a rhythm to the work, Paul started to relax. It felt good to be back working under the sun after so many days lying on a mattress. If I can keep working like this all day, he thought, I'll show Matthew that he made a good decision when he purchased me.

Paul had removed the bark on less than half the log when Matthew appeared by his side. "It takes practice. Don't expect to be as fast as I am right away. I'll finish this side. You go to the second log and start stripping off the bark. By the time we finish with all three, you'll be almost as fast as I am."

Paul was halfway done when he noticed Matthew picking up a saw. At once, his master began cutting straight across the top of the trunk he'd been working on, starting about two feet from the end. He cut until the saw's teeth reached the edge of the bark they'd left on the log. Then Matthew moved the saw two feet down the log's length and made another cut like the first one. Finished, he moved down again and started a third cut. After watching Matthew carefully for a few minutes, Paul went back to work.

When Matthew was done, he climbed on top of the log with his adze. Standing about two feet back from one end, he raised the heavy tool above his head and swung its sharp blade into the top of one of the cuts he'd made, carving away a flat section of wood. Matthew kept cutting with the adze, carefully alternated his cuts between each side of the log. Soon he'd removed the top wood, carving out a flat section about six inches deep and three feet across. With that done, he stepped back along the top of the log and began cutting the next section in the same manner.

Matthew continued swinging the adze until he'd cut a flat section along the entire length of the trunk. "Paul" he called out, "I need two planks from the shed. Bring them here."

When Paul returned with the first plank, he saw that Matthew had placed a large, flat rock several inches back from the bottom of the felled trunk. Paul understood immediately as his master wedged an end of the plank as far beneath the log as he could manage. They were going to use the two planks and stones as levers to roll the log in the same way they'd done when they first built the raft on the Severn River. Paul returned with the second plank and placed one end under the opposite end of the log. Matthew did the same with the second rock and plank.

"Now we'll turn it until the section I've just flattened is resting on the ground. Pull down on your plank!"

Their first try only moved the flat side part-way toward the ground. Paul and Matthew moved the rocks closer to the log and used their planks to roll it again. On the third try, the flat portion rested in the dirt.

"That section will be the top of this new canoe. With it resting on the ground, the log will not roll anymore. We can stop now and see if Mary has our midday meal ready."

Paul was surprised the morning had passed so quickly. He felt good to be working again and to be learning how to turn a thirty-foot log into a sailing canoe. But he also felt exhausted. He was ready to rest and go back to the cabin for food.

Mary looked at Paul closely when he entered the cabin, but she didn't say anything. Matthew and Paul took their bowls of salt pork stew and walked back outside to sit in the sun with their backs against the cabin wall. Susan and Mary joined them. They all watched little Martha playing in the dirt in front of the cabin's door.

After eating, Matthew studied Paul for a few moments. Then, satisfied that the boy was fit enough to go back to work, he stood and said, "Come along, Paul. It's time to get back to the boatyard."

When Matthew and Paul returned to the boatyard, Paul picked up his hatchet and started to remove the bark from the third log. "Leave that log for now," said Matthew, "and come over here to watch what I do."

Matthew continued: "The side of the log that now is on top will become the bottom of the canoe. First we'll remove the remaining bark. When that's done, I'll use my hatchet and the adze to cut away the wood along each side of the bottom. I'll leave a two-inch-wide section that runs straight from one end to the other to form the keel."

"What's a keel?" asked Paul.

"The keel is a solid section of wood at the exact bottom of the canoe. It runs from the bow to the stern. It's a critical part of the canoe's shape. It keeps the canoe moving in a straight line when you're rowing it through the water. You'll see why after I've carved it out of the log."

"Go back to the shed. Bring me the board that's as tall as you and about three fingers wide. That will be my guide for cutting out the keel."

Paul found the guide resting against the shed wall where Matthew kept his tools. When he returned, Matthew had removed most of the remaining bark on one side. Paul picked up his hatchet and started to remove the bark on the other side.

Matthew set the wooden guide on the top of the log and with his hatchet began to cut out notches of wood along both sides of the guide. When he'd cut away about three inches of wood on opposite sides of his guide, he moved it down to the next section of the log and repeated the process.

Paul was amazed at how fast Matthew worked and at how much control he had with the hatchet. After Matthew had moved the guide five times, Paul could see the wooden keel beginning to emerge along the center of the log.

"Getting the keel right is the most important part of carving out the canoe. It has to be straight from one end to the other. It has to be deep enough to keep the canoe from turning when the wind comes across the water and hits the bow or stern. Now go back to that third log and finish removing the bark from both sides. While you do that, I'll use the adze to cut away the rest of the wood and shape the bottom of this canoe."

Paul and Matthew continued to work in silence. When the sun touched the top of the trees at the edge of the boatyard, Paul could feel his arms and shoulders aching. He was happy when Matthew told him to gather up the tools and return them to the shed.

"We've many more days ahead of us before this canoe is ready for the water," Matthew said. "But I can tell you take to working with these tools quickly. You watch what I do very carefully. With luck, we'll have three canoes finished by September. If we do, we can take them back to Battle Creek to sell, and get orders for more to build during the winter."

9

Return to Battle Town

Matthew steered his sailing canoe out of the broad, clear waters of the Patuxent River into the mouth of Battle Creek. As the vessel made a gentle curve through the quiet water, Paul looked back at the three new canoes they'd pulled behind them all the way from South River. Paul felt proud of the work they'd done carving the canoes out of those thirty-foot pine logs in Matthew's boatyard. He'd learned so much from Matthew. He'd grown stronger and more confident through the long summer days cutting away the pine to reveal the sleek shapes gliding through the water behind them.

The trees surrounding Battle Town were beginning to take on their fall colors. Reds and yellows marked the maples that grew among the pin oaks and pines. Deep copper tones were building on the beech trees at the edge of the forest.

This land is more beautiful than I ever imagined, thought Paul, as they sailed toward the wharf. It didn't seem so beautiful when he'd sailed out of Battle Creek last spring and left Rebecca behind in the inn. Paul remembered how hard those days had been. Perhaps, he mused, our lives will be good here after all.

The many weeks of summer had gone by quickly. At first Paul was disappointed that he couldn't spend all day with Matthew. Besides his morning chores, he had to work in the fields with his hoe cutting grasses and weeds away from the corn stalks. When that was done, he'd hurry to join Matthew in the boatyard.

When August came and the corn started to ripen, Paul had to spend more hours with Mary picking beans, pulling corn from the stalks, and carrying baskets filled with their harvest back to the cabin. Susan was so heavy with child she couldn't work in the fields and take care of Martha at the same time. So she remained in the cabin and prepared the beans and corn for winter storage.

To get more time in the boatyard, Paul began to get up before sunrise to do his cabin chores so that he could get out to the fields at first light. Mary started leaving him a bowl of food from the prior evening's meal because he was away from the cabin before she'd have time to cook. Paul didn't mind the cold meal. He enjoyed working in the fields in the cool of the morning. By working fast, he'd finish and get to the canoes about the same time as Matthew.

In the boatyard, Paul learned to use the wood planes to smooth the outer sides of each canoe after Matthew had carved out its shape with the hatchet. Matthew shaped each side by eye, stepping back from the log from time to time to make sure he was removing the right amount of wood from each section of the canoe. When Matthew completed one side, Paul would remove the rough edges and ridges with a plane. When he was done, the canoe had a smooth curve that would glide easily through the water.

When the outer sides were finished, they'd turn the canoe over and place blocks of wood on either side of the keel to hold the half-finished craft upright. Matthew would use his hatchet and adze to carve out the wood from inside the canoe, leaving enough wood in the bow to shape a solid section that could be carved into a mount for the mast.

After working together for the first month, Matthew realized he could leave Paul to work alone on the canoes while he attended to other things. Some days he'd check on the progress of his tenants raising tobacco on 150 acres of land he owned on South River. Twice he sailed alone to the Severn to check on the crop there.

As a landowner, Matthew had to serve on juries when the local court was called into session. Captain William Burdett, who owned most of the land along South River, was the senior judge for their small community. When court was in session, he'd send word to Matthew to appear at his home where he convened the court. As a landowner, Matthew had to attend and serve as a member of the jury deciding the cases. Most cases involved disputes about land boundaries between plantation owners. Some were about monies owed by planters who'd borrowed from ship captains or tobacco factors with a promise to pay with their next harvest. If the harvest was poor and debts accumulated, the court might order the planter to sell some land to settle the debt.

When Paul was working alone, he liked to spend time carving oars for the canoes from eight-foot maple timbers Matthew cut for that purpose. With a drawing knife and the wood planes, Paul would shape the flat section of the oar the rower would dip into the water. Then he'd shape the handle. With both ends formed, he'd round the remaining length of the oar's shaft to give it a smooth and finished look.

"Paul," said Matthew as they sailed further into Battle Creek, "we're going to row the remaining distance. With these three canoes in tow, we can't sail right up to the wharf. When I let the sail drift free in the wind, put the oars between their pins on the gunnels and bring the bow straight into the wind. I'll move to the bow to drop the sail and row with the other set of oars when everything is secure."

Soon Matthew and Paul had the canoes secured to the Battle Town wharf. Paul again looked at the crafts with pride. One was equipped as a sailing canoe, with two sets of oars, a mast and pole for rigging the sail. The new owner would have to purchase the sail and ropes from one of the ships' captains who traded here in Battle Town. Aside from that, the craft was complete.

The other two canoes were designed to carry hogsheads of tobacco from upriver plantations down to Battle Creek. For these canoes, Matthew had eliminated more of the wood from the bow because they would not require a place to mount the mast for the sail. To leave room for the hogsheads in the middle of the canoe, Paul had set the wooden pegs that would guide the oars used in the bow further forward than their placement in the sailing canoe. The rowing canoes wouldn't sell for as much as a sailing canoe. But there was great demand for them up and down Battle Creek and on the Patuxent.

"Why don't you go to the Punch to see your sister," said Matthew, when the canoes were secured to the wharf. "I'm going to the home of Michael Taney. He's promised to purchase the sailing canoe, and will know the planters in need of the rowing canoes. If I can't sell these other two right away, Taney will act as my agent, sell them for me and keep twenty shillings for each. When I'm finished with Taney, I'll join you at the inn."

Paul was out of the canoe and moving down the wharf before Matthew could complete his last sentence. He couldn't wait to see the surprise on his sister's face. He had so much to tell Rebecca about his new life on South River, the work in the boatyard, and Matthew and his family.

When he walked through the door of the Punch, Rebecca was cleaning around the tables and sweeping the floor. Since it was too early for the evening meals, they were alone in the inn. "Rebecca," called out Paul.

Rebecca turned toward the voice in the doorway.

"Rebecca, I'm back. It's just like I promised. I've come back to see you. Now put down that broom and come to greet your brother!"

Rebecca dropped the broom. "Paul, oh Paul, what are you doing here?" Before she could say another word, Paul crossed the room and put his arms around his sister. Rebecca started to cry.

"Please, Rebecca, stop your crying. Come sit with me here. I've come with Matthew to sell canoes. We'll leave again soon so we can get back to South River. I've so much to tell you. Let's use the short time we have and feel joy that we're together again."

He led Rebecca to one of the tables and began telling her about all that had happened since he left Battle Town with Matthew. He talked about sailing on the Chesapeake and falling ill to the seasoning. He described Mary and Susan and Matthew's young daughter, Martha. And he talked and talked about the boatyard, the canoes and all he'd learned.

Rebecca listened silently to her brother. Her expression didn't change. She neither smiled nor asked questions.

Finally Paul stopped. "What about you, here at the Punch?"

Rebecca began to cry again. "Paul, please take me away. It's so hard here. I must work from sunrise until all of the customers have left the inn or retired to their sleeping room. Even then I have to stay here and clean until everything is ready for the morning. If I stop, Master Cosgrove yells at me or punishes me. Only the cook, Mama Ailsworth, is kind to me."

Rebecca continued pouring out her heart to Paul, with tears flowing down her face.

At first Paul thought she just needed to tell him her troubles. But as Rebecca's stories about her hard life in the inn continued, Paul began to feel very sad for his sister and for the differences between her life and his. When Rebecca stopped talking, Paul sat silently staring at her tears. He didn't know what to say. He didn't know what to do.

"Please, please, please take me away with you," Rebecca pleaded again.

"He can't take you away," said Matthew, who had come into the inn and walked quietly to where Rebecca and Paul were sitting. "If you run away from your master, you'll be caught and punished. The judges can add more years to the time you have to serve Cosgrove for running away."

"But sir," stammered Rebecca, "my life here is so hard. I can't stay here.

I'll die. Please, sir, help me. Please. Won't you and my brother help me?"

"If Paul or I try to help you, we'll be punished too. Now go back to your work. Paul and I have to begin our journey back to South River to reach there before night falls. We'll return in six months. Paul will spend more time with you then."

Rebecca looked at Matthew. She looked at Paul. Her face fell blank. Slowly, she rose up from the table and moved away from her brother. Before Paul could say anything, she began to sob and rushed through the rear door and out of the inn.

Paul rose from the table and walked over to Matthew, who turned and walked out of the inn. As they made their way to the wharf, Paul remembered how he felt the first time they'd left Battle Town. Once again he felt confused. Once again he was angry. He was angry with Matthew. He was angry with himself for not being able to protect his sister. As he walked slowly to the wharf, he knew it'd be a long, hard sail back to South River.

draw knife

Becoming a Burgess

The months before the first snow were busier on South River than the long days of summer. Matthew's tenants were hard at work harvesting their tobacco, stripping the leaves from the tall plants and drying them on the ground. After the September sun turned the leaves brown, they carried the tobacco into special sheds where the leaves would be strung together and hung on poles to dry throughout the winter months.

The strong, pungent smell of tobacco surrounded the sheds in the warm days of October, making the men think of the money they'd earn when they sold their 600 pound hogsheads filled with the cured tobacco to English captains in the spring.

Paul, Mary, and Matthew finished harvesting their corn and gathered all of the squash that had grown among the beans and corn throughout the summer. While Mary stored away the squash in a shed attached to the cabin, Paul and Matthew picked the year's crop of apples and brought them to the cider press. There they pressed the apples into liquid and stored the fresh cider in large kegs. Its sweet smell permeated their clothes with a promise of many satisfying drinks throughout the coming year. Matthew buried one small cask in a hole outside his cabin where it would slowly turn to alcohol over the winter months.

In the middle of the fall harvest, Susan, so heavy with her soon to be born child that she could not work, finally went into labor. Paul awoke that morning to the sound of Susan calling to Mary from her sleeping room upstairs. Matthew suddenly came below, lifted the heavy kettle from its iron hook where it hung over the fire and carried it out the cabin door. "You get more wood for the fire," Matthew yelled to Paul. "I'll get more water. Mary wants this kettle boiling as soon as possible."

As Paul moved toward the door, he heard Susan cry out again. When he returned with his arms full of wood, Matthew was placing the kettle back on its hook over the fire. Mary came down from Susan's room, carrying Martha with her. "Now you two get out of the cabin," Mary commanded, "and take Martha with you. I don't have time to cook for you this morning. Matthew, take these two to the inn by Captain Burdett's wharf and buy them some food. Then find something useful to do, but don't come back here until the sun's set. I'll have enough to do this day without having to worry about you getting in the way."

Again Susan cried out. Paul looked at Matthew, who simply took Martha by the hand and walked out of the cabin door. Paul hurried to catch up with them. "What will happen to Susan?" he asked.

Matthew laughed and gave Paul a look that the young boy hadn't seen before. "Don't worry about Susan. Just mind what Mary said and stay out of her way this day. Mary's attended the birth of nearly every child born on this side of the river since we came here from the Severn. Whenever a woman goes into labor, she sends her husband to fetch Mary. Right now, I'll bet she's mixing some cider with special roots and plants to help Susan ease the birth. The only danger is to anyone who interferes with Mary at a time like this."

Matthew's words were true. When they returned to the cabin at the day's end, Mary greeted them with Matthew's new son in her arms. "Go up to see your wife," she said to Matthew, "but don't stay too long. It was a hard birth and she's weak. She must rest for the next few days and tend to her son. When you're done, come back down to hold this fine, strong child. You'll be sleeping down here with Paul for the next week so Susan can rest. I'll take Martha with me into my sleeping room."

Over the following weeks, the DaSilva family's routine slowly returned to normal. Mary was back at the fireplace, preparing the family's meals. Whenever she had time, she would climb the stairs to look in on Susan, who remained weak from the difficult labor and birth. Little Martha spent more time with her grandmother, who patiently tried to teach her how to prepare food and clean the cabin. For several weeks, all Susan could do was nurse her son. Finally she was strong enough to come down the stairs and help Mary any way she could.

Matthew and Paul went back to the boatyard. Matthew was excited about the work they'd do that winter. He'd sold the three canoes in Battle Town for thirty pounds sterling, which was twice what a tobacco planter and his family could earn in a year when the crop was good. With some of the money he purchased a cow and an ox. The cow would add to the food supply for his growing family. With the ox he'd pull more logs and lumber from his land on the South River, and then lease it to planters for work in their fields. He planned to double the production of canoes now that he had Paul working with him.

Just after New Year, Matthew was called to a meeting of landowners at Captain Burdett's home. He left Paul to carve new oars for the canoes they'd build from the four pine logs now sitting in the yard. It was late morning when Matthew returned.

Paul expected Matthew to tell him to begin working on the first pine log. Instead, Matthew walked over to where Paul was using the drawing knife to shape the long shaft of an oar. For several minutes, Matthew just watched Paul work. "You've learned that skill well. I can't tell the difference between oars I'd make and the one you're carving today. But can you carve a canoe out of one of these logs on your own? That's the question we'll have to ask when this next year's tobacco and corn have been planted."

Paul didn't understand Matthew's meaning. He started to ask, but then stopped. He knew by now that it was better to wait for Matthew to talk than to press him with questions. So he continued drawing the blade against the maple shaft to finish the oar.

"I'm now this area's burgess," said Matthew. "Captain Burdett has been appointed by Lord Baltimore to serve on his Privy Council. That means he becomes an advisor to the Governor and one of the most important men in Maryland. As a member of the Privy Council, he can no longer represent this area's landowners in the colony's Assembly. South River needs someone in the Assembly to make sure any new laws created by Lord Baltimore and his Governor for the colony will not place too great a hardship on us."

Paul could see from Matthew's expression that something important had happened. But he didn't really understand what Matthew had said. What was a burgess? When Matthew stopped talking, Paul decided he better ask. "What does that mean for you?"

"Today he nominated me to take his place in the Assembly, and my fellow landowners elected me as their burgess. That means I'll represent all of the landowners on South River when new laws are debated in the Assembly. Next summer, when I would have been working with you in this boatyard, I'll travel to St. Mary's City for a meeting of the Assembly."

Paul could tell by Matthew's voice that he was pleased by this honor. He continued working in silence, hoping Matthew would tell him more.

"At first, I asked Captain Burdett to nominate another landowner. But he argued that I was the best choice for this area, pointing out that the other landowners had to work their tobacco fields alongside their family and indentured servants. Since I've tenants on my land and a productive boatyard to add to my income, I can afford to be away for the time when the Assembly's in session.

"Burdett also took me aside and explained that members of the Assembly can count on being appointed by the Governor to other official positions, and those carry an annual income from the tax revenues.

"So Paul, we'll have to work hard this winter to build as many canoes as possible. When I'm away at the Assembly, you'll be in charge of the boatyard. I know you'll be able to produce oars, masts, and poles for the sails. We'll see if you're ready by summer to carve a canoe on your own."

Paul continued to work quietly. He didn't want Matthew to see how excited he was by this news. He'd be on his own for some time next summer. He'd show Matthew what he could produce by himself.

11

Taney's Dilemma

Rebecca hurried to clear away the dishes after the evening meal. With only one person staying in the inn that night, she hoped she could get the floors swept and everything put away early. If Cosgrove didn't stay late drinking with the planter who'd come to Battle Town to purchase supplies, she could go to bed early and get some rest.

Suddenly the inn's front door swung open and Michael Taney rushed into the room. "Cosgrove," shouted Taney, "where's your wife? She must come to my home right away. My wife has taken to her bed. She is barely breathing and can't even open her eyes. I fear she's dying. Your wife must come to see to her right away!"

Cosgrove looked across at Taney, straining to keep any emotion from his face. Damn this man, he thought. Who does he think he is to come into my inn and order me to send my wife as if she's a servant in his household.

But he held his tongue. He knew better than to speak in anger to Taney, the second most powerful man in the area.

"My wife, sir, can't be of aid to you," said Cosgrove, as he rose slowly from the table and walked toward Taney. "We'd gladly help. But she knows nothing about caring for the sick and injured. She might do your wife more harm than good if she goes to her bedside."

"Than what about the African who cooks for you and your guests?"

"You mean Mama Allsworth?"

"Yes. That's the one. Baker Brooke tells me she was the one person his father trusted when anyone in his household fell ill or was injured. As much as I hate the idea that someone of her kind would touch my wife, I'm desperate. My wife may not last the week without someone to care for her. If she dies, I'll be left with no one to raise my children. Bringing a new wife over from England is expensive and a risky business."

Cosgrove felt cornered by Taney. Confound this man, he thought. What right does he have to interfere with my business?

But he paused before answering. He didn't want his wife to appear as someone's servant, required to work in Taney's home. But he didn't want to lose his cook to this man either. The inn depended on her work and skill.

"Mama Allsworth has gone to her home for the night," said Cosgrove. "And tomorrow I'll need her in the inn to cook. Remember there will be a court session in two days. Planters will be coming for the trials. My inn will be full."

"And my wife will be dead," said Taney in response. "How can you think about your business when I need your cook to care for my wife?"

At that moment, Cosgrove caught sight of Rebecca sweeping around the tables. Perhaps, he thought, I can avoid Taney's anger without losing my cook.

"What about my girl servant, Rebecca? I can spare her for a few days. You can take her back with you and instruct her in caring for your wife."

Taney looked at Rebecca, and turned back toward Cosgrove with anger rising in his eyes. "Do you mock me, sir? My wife faces death. Do you think I know how to care for her? And what can that scrawny, uneducated child do?"

"I don't mean that Rebecca will cure your wife," responded Cosgrove, quickly. "I'll also send for Mama Allsworth and tell her to go to your home to care for your wife. Mama can teach Rebecca what to do and still work as my cook. Rebecca will do anything Mama says. And I'll let Mama go to see your wife several times each day so that she can make sure the child is doing the right things."

Taney stood silent for a few moments. He looked again at Rebecca, then back at Cosgrove. The anger still flickered in his eyes, but his voice was cold and steely when finally he spoke. "Alright, inn keeper. If that's the best you can offer. But I promise you, I will not forget this night. If my wife dies, you will not forget it either. Now send for your cook. Tell her to go to the swamp before she comes to my home so she can bring leeches with her. Bleeding my wife may be the only way to save her. I fear some evil spirits have entered her body. Your cook must drain out this evil as quickly as possible."

With his threat still hanging in the air, Taney turned and walked out of the inn.

Cosgrove turned to Rebecca. "Quick, girl, go get Mama Allsworth. Tell her to gather leeches and go to Taney's house as soon as possible. And you pay careful attention to what Mama Allsworth tells you to do. If Taney's wife dies, it will be you who answers to his anger."

12

Lessons for Rebecca

Rebecca was nearly out of breath when she reached Mama Allsworth's door. "Mama," she called out, "come quickly. I need you."

Mama opened her door and pulled Rebecca inside. "Becca, what is it? Has Cosgrove done something to you again?"

"No Mama, it's not Cosgrove. It's Master Taney. He says his wife is sick and may die. Cosgrove wants you to go to Taney's home and care for her. If she dies, Taney says he will punish Cosgrove. The innkeeper says I'll be to blame if that happens. Please protect me."

"Hush, Becca. Quiet your fears. You know I won't let Cosgrove harm you. But that's not our worry now. We must find out what's wrong with Mrs. Taney. If she's that close to death, we must move quickly."

"Master Taney said that you should first go to the swamp to get leeches. He wants you to bleed the evil out of his wife."

"Bleed his wife? What does that man know? First we must see Mrs. Taney. We'll not know what to do until I can look at her eyes, watch her breathe, and feel her skin. It could be what they call the seasoning. It could be what they call consumption. We won't know until we get there, and we can't help her standing here in my house."

With that, Mama Allsworth reached for a leather sack hanging on the back of her door, threw a blanket across her shoulders, took Rebecca by the hand, and headed her out into the night. As they hurried along the path towards the inn and Master Taney's house, Rebecca looked at Mama in wonder.

"Do you know how to cure her?"

"I won't know until we see her."

"Where did you learn how to cure people? Are you a physician and a cook?"

"I'm no physician, Becca. But I know a few things about caring for others. Some things I learned in Master Brooke's household. In England I'd watch the physicians when they'd treat Master Brooke and his children. I also learned long ago, when I was a child, not much older than you. I learned from my mother and from her mother too. My mother's mother was a great healer in our village. She could go into the forest and find plants and roots and other living things that could end fevers, stop bleeding and ease the pains of childbirth. So we'll see if I can help Mrs. Taney. If you watch me carefully, and do as I say, you'll learn some of these things too. But promise not to tell anyone what we do. Many people in Battle Town believe in evil spirits and evil magic. I keep what I know secret so no one can accuse me of working with the devil."

Mama's words worried Rebecca. But she trusted her. She'd tell no one. Still, she thought, if Mrs. Taney died, would we be blamed? What will Master Taney and Cosgrove do to us then?

These questions occupied her thoughts as Rebecca and Mama came to Taney's home. Not stopping to knock, Mama opened the door and pulled Rebecca with her into the main room.

Rebecca stood still. She'd never been inside a place like this. The room was filled with light from candles burning on every wall. The tables and chairs were smooth and solid, reflecting the candlelight in their polished surfaces. On one wall she saw a portrait of Master Taney and next to it was a portrait of his wife. There were pewter plates on shelves behind a large table that had eight high-backed chairs around it.

Rebecca was about to say something to Mama when Master Taney entered the room.

"My wife's back here in our bedroom," he said. "She's barely breathing. Go to her quickly."

Mama walked past Taney without saying a word. When Rebecca entered the bedroom, her eyes took a few minutes to adjust to the darkness. Only one candle burned on the table next to the bed. As her eyes grew accustomed to the dim light, Rebecca was amazed again. Mrs. Taney lay on a bed that was as long as one of the tables in the inn and twice as wide. She lay on a mattress that was lifted by the bed frame almost three feet off the floor. Four poles rose from the four corners, holding up a cloth canopy as long and wide as the bed itself.

"Come over here, Becca," said Mama in a low whisper. "Tell me what you see."

Rebecca hesitated. Mrs. Taney looked awful. Her face was white. She didn't appear to be breathing. Rebecca's first thought was they were too late. "Is she dead?"

"No, Becca, she's not dead yet. Come closer and put your hand just above her mouth. Do you feel her breath? She's still breathing, but it's very slow and weak. Now touch her forehead. Tell me what you feel."

"Her forehead is wet, but it also feels cold."

"That's right. It means she doesn't have a fever. So we know she's not suffering from the seasoning. Now take your right fingers and place it on your left wrist, just under the inside of your hand. Do you feel anything under your fingers?"

At first Rebecca couldn't feel anything. But as she pressed her fingers down harder, she began to feel something push back against it."

"Do you feel something pushing against the tips of your fingers? That, Rebecca, is your life force. Tell me what it feels like."

"It feels like there's something inside tapping. There's a tap, then nothing, then another tap, then nothing. Then another tap like the way rain drops fall from the side of a house."

"Now press your fingers on the same place on Mrs. Taney's left wrist, just below her hand. What do you feel?"

"I can feel a tap. Then there's nothing. Then three or four taps go quickly, then nothing again. Then a tap again, followed by eight or nine in a row, like something racing up her wrist. What does that mean?"

"Her life force isn't steady. Something's disturbing it. That's why it feels like something racing inside her."

"Is that why she's dying? Can you save her?"

At first Mama didn't answer. She moved over to the table with the candle and opened up the leather pouch she'd carried from her home. Out came a short stick, rounded at the end. Out came a small bowl. Out came some small packets of paper, which Mama carefully set down by the bowl.

"Now Becca, go out to Master Taney and get him to show you where he keeps the clean water they use for cooking. Bring me about four cups of water and one of the metal cups they use in the cooking area."

Rebecca raced out of the bedroom and almost ran into Taney, who was pacing back and forth in front of the portraits on the wall. "Please sir, show me where your wife prepares the food."

Taney looked at the girl in surprise. He'd never heard her talk. Now she was asking for his help. Without taking his eye from Rebecca, he pointed to a door at the far end of the room. Rebecca understood right away and ran through the door.

In less than a minute, Rebecca was back in the bedroom, standing next to Mama, with a small bucket of water and a metal drinking cup. She watched as Mama opened up one of the packets and put its contents into the bowl she'd placed next to the candle.

"Put half a cup of water into that bowl, Becca. Now watch as I mix the powder from the packet into the water. When you can't see any of the powder, add another half cup of water to the bowl."

"What are you mixing into the water," asked Rebecca?

"I'm mixing the dried flowers and seeds from a plant the English call Foxglove. When I'm finished, we'll pour it into Mrs. Taney's mouth slowly so she swallows without choking."

"What will it do?"

"I can't be sure that it will work. But I've seen this Foxglove powder help people whose life force is disturbed this way. Now lift her head up and pull down her jaw so I can pour this mixture into her mouth."

Rebecca didn't like to touch this woman who seemed so close to death. But she knew Mama was her only hope, and finally did what she had been instructed.

"Now Becca, this first mixture probably will not be enough. We'll have to give her the powder in water several times before this night is over. I have to get some sleep if I'm going to cook for Cosgrove all day tomorrow. So here's what you're going to do. You'll stay here, mix up another packet of powder with water, and then give it to Mrs. Taney three more times before sunrise. Do you think you can mix the powder just the way I did?"

"Yes, Mama. But how will I know when to give her the next drink?"

"You'll know by the candle. Watch."

Rebecca watched as Mama took out a small knife from a pocket just below her waist. Taking the burning candle by its holder, Mama cut a shallow circle around it about halfway down from the burning wick. Then she picked up another candle that was lying on the table. She marked the second candle in the middle and set it on the table.

"When this candle burns down to the place where I've cut, it will be time to give Mrs. Taney another drink of water with the powder. When this first candle is about to burn out, light the second candle and put it into the holder. Then give Mrs. Taney another drink of the powder and water. When the second candle burns down to the place I've marked, give her the third drink. By then it will almost be daylight. I'll come back to check on you and Mrs. Taney before I go to the inn. This poor woman will either start improving by morning or we'll have to tell her husband nothing can save her."

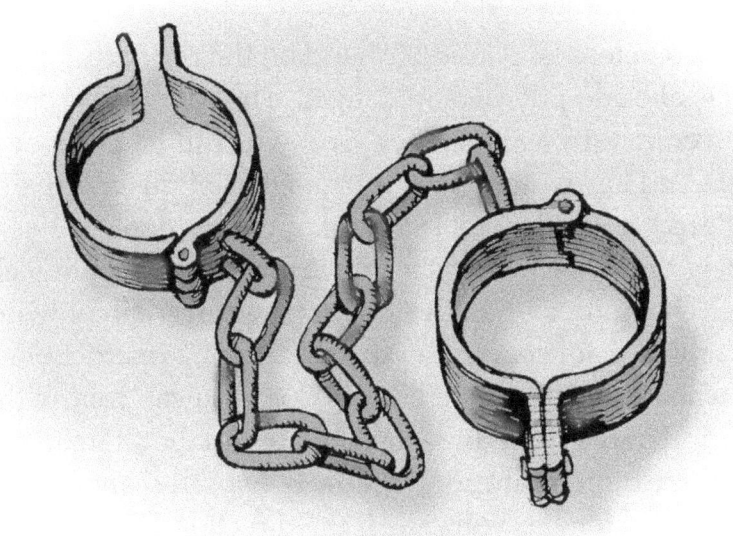

13

Returning to Battle Town

SPRING 1673 — The new tobacco plants were growing in their seedbeds when Matthew and Paul loaded 1,000 board feet of lumber for Captain Darby into three canoes they'd built over the winter. Matthew used short lengths of rope to tie the three canoes together in a row, pushing each canoe in turn out into South River. Then he tied a rope to the stern of his sailing canoe, linking it to the canoes loaded with the lumber.

"Now," he said to Paul, "we're ready for our journey to Battle Creek. We'll use the oars to row out into the river. Then we'll set the sail and let the wind drive us down the Bay." As the sun rose above the oaks at the edge of the boatyard, they slowly rowed out into South River. Fortunately, the spring winds were strong. As soon as the sail was up, the wind seemed to pick up the canoe, driving them and the convoy of rowing canoes in tow behind them rapidly down the Bay.

Paul was happy when the morning sun began to warm his body as it rose higher in the clear sky. The Bay waters still held the cold of winter, and the icy wind reached deep inside his clothing as they made their way south toward the Patuxent River.

When they reached the mouth of the Patuxent, Matthew turned to Paul.

"It's time you learn to sail. You take control of the rudder. I'll control the sail. Keep the wind coming toward the canoe so it strikes the right side of your face. Move the rudder's handle very gently and watch how the canoe turns in response."

Paul hesitated before he placed his hand on the rudder's handle, fearing he'd make a mistake and put them in danger. The water was cold. If the canoe tipped over in a strong gust, they'd drown. But he knew he had to obey Matthew. And his excitement at learning to sail pushed against his fear.

Taking a deep breath, Paul took control of the rudder.

Immediately the canoe moved as if it were alive. He could feel the craft's motion through the rudder's handle. The smallest movement would swing the bow right or left. Paul concentrated on Matthew's instructions.

Matthew watched the boy carefully. "When you can control the canoe and keep the wind in the right direction, look out to the shoreline over the bow and pick a tree directly ahead. Aim the bow of the canoe at that tree. Stay on that course as long as you can. If the direction of the wind changes, find a new mark on the shoreline and aim for that place. I'll adjust the sail to keep us moving."

After several minutes Paul looked out across the bow and found a tree far down the shoreline. That was his target. The minutes dragged by like hours as he concentrated on staying on course. Finally he started to breathe easily again. He was sailing.

Paul steered and Matthew controlled the sail until they reached the mouth of Battle Creek. "I'll take over," said Matthew. "With the three canoes trailing behind, turning into the Creek will take careful handling. When we're safely into the Creek, I'll release the sail and drop it down the mast. You use the oars to steer us directly into the wind. When the sail is down, I'll use the oars in the bow and we'll row to shore."

With Matthew at the second set of oars, it didn't take long to reach Battle Town's wharf. Once the four canoes were safely tied to the wharf, Matthew turned to Paul. "I know you want to see your sister right away. Go off to the Punch. I'll go to speak with Taney about selling these canoes and storing this lumber until Captain Darby brings the *Providence* back to Battle Creek for this year's tobacco. When I'm done, I'll join you at the inn."

Paul didn't hesitate. He moved quickly up the ladder and across the wharf toward the inn. He was worried about Rebecca, but eager to see her again. As he walked toward the inn, his mind cast back to their last meeting. Rebecca's life seemed so hard. If only they could be together again, some place where he could help her and protect her. His heart felt heavy as he slowly made his way from the wharf.

When he reached the inn, it was filled with men sitting silently at the tables. Next to the fireplace, five men sat facing out toward the crowd. Paul looked for Rebecca. He found her standing against the wall on the far right side of the room. She looked up and caught Paul's eye. Is that fear, Paul thought, as he tried to read the expression on her face? What could be wrong now?

Nervously, Paul made his way through the crowd over toward Rebecca until he was standing next to her. "What's happening here?"

"It's a trial. That's the chief judge, Baker Brooke, sitting at the center of the table. Michael Taney and my master, Thomas Cosgrove, are sitting next to him. The other two men are planters who live at the head of the Creek. They're all the judges."

"Who are the men standing in front of the judges?"

"One of them is Battle Town's constable, who's in charge of the prisoner. The other is Timothy McNeely who sailed with us from London on the *Providence* and was purchased by Taney."

At that moment, Matthew appeared next to Rebecca and Paul. "They told me at Taney's home he was here for the trial of a servant. What's the charge?"

"Timothy McNeely," called out the chief judge, "you're accused of running away from the plantation where your master, Michael Taney, placed you to work, and with stealing food and clothing when you ran from his service. How do you answer this charge?"

"I ran because the plantation overseer beat me," replied McNeely, unable to hide the anger in his voice. "For the first months he locked me in a shed with chains on my feet each night. When I was working in the fields, he'd hit me with his whip if I stopped to get water. Some days he'd deny me food when the others stopped to eat. He gave better care to the hogs and his dogs."

"Michael Taney," said the chief judge, "you're this man's master. What do you say?"

Taney rose from his chair, confidently placing a hand on the shoulder of the chief judge. "My friends, I thank you for hearing my case today. It's a simple matter. When I purchased this man from Captain Darby, the good captain warned me McNeely was a thief and not to be trusted. I sent him to my plantation on the Patuxent where my overseer is stern but fair. I hoped this man would change his ways and earn his freedom through hard work and obedience.

"You hear him admit he's tried to deny me my right to his labor by running away and has stolen food and clothing from my plantation. I ask the court for justice and proper punishment of this man."

After Taney finished, the chief judge looked briefly to his left and then to his right.

"I've consulted with my fellow judges. We all find you, Timothy McNeely, guilty of flight and theft. As punishment, I add one more year of service to your indenture. To let others know of your crimes, your right hand will be branded with the letter T to mark you as a thief. I warn you to change your ways. If you come before this court again, we'll not treat you so lightly for your crimes."

With the sentence announced, the men in the room filed out of the inn and walked toward the town's jail to watch the constable place the branding iron on McNeely's hand. Public punishment was a popular event in the town.

Rebecca slowly turned to Paul. "I feared this Timothy McNeely," she said in almost a whisper as if afraid others would hear. "He was cruel during our voyage. But burning his flesh as punishment? What kind of men are our masters?"

Before Paul could speak, Matthew answered her. "An indentured servant is the property of his master until he completes his service. He owes his labor to his master and must be obedient in all things. This brand on his hand will be a sign to other servants that they must do what they're told and work hard to repay their master."

Paul was surprised by the harsh tone in his master's voice. Out of the corner of his eye, he could see that Matthew's words were affecting Rebecca too.

"We can't have order in this colony if we allow bad fellows like McNeely to get away with their crimes," continued Matthew. "Perhaps he'll learn from this punishment and remember every day when he looks at this mark that he must do what Taney commands.

"Now I have to talk with Taney and conclude my business here in Battle Town. Paul, you can visit with your sister until her master calls her back to work. Then come to the wharf to help me unload the lumber and store it in Taney's warehouse."

Paul and Rebecca moved to a table. He watched his sister for a moment, sensing her fear was more than the punishment. "How are you Rebecca? How is your life in Battle Town?"

Rebecca did not answer right away. She looked at her brother, wondering if she could tell the truth. If she told him about Cosgrove's switch and how hard she had to work each day, would Paul be able to do anything about it? Probably not.

"Life is hard here, Paul. My master is not like your master. But at least I have Mama Allsworth to teach me and help me. She and I saved the life of Master Taney's wife, and for that Master Taney spoke well of me to my master. But the innkeeper only thanked Master Taney for his kind words. As soon as Taney left, my master called me a lazy, useless girl and yelled at me to get back to work. Now I see what they'll do if we don't obey. I fear the innkeeper will have me branded some day."

As Rebecca finished sharing her fears, Cosgrove came back into the inn. "Why are you sitting there, you lazy girl? Get back to work. Do I have to ask the judge to reconvene the court to make you obey?"

Before Paul could speak, Rebecca rose from the table and hurried out the back door of the inn. "And you, boy," continued Cosgrove, "why are you interferring here in my inn. Get back to your master where you belong."

Paul didn't know what to say. But he knew better than to speak against the innkeeper. Slowly he rose from the table and walked toward the front door, keeping his head down so as not to look Cosgrove in the eye.

As he walked toward the wharf, his mind kept returning to Rebecca's last words. He knew Rebecca would think often about McNeely and the brand burned into his flesh. Could he and Matthew do anything to protect her?

As he neared the wharf with questions swirling in his mind, he saw that Matthew was still engaged in conversation with Taney. Knowing better than to interrupt, Paul stood quietly to the side, half listening to the two men.

"Paul," called Matthew. "Come here. Master Taney has something to tell you."

"I just told your master, the boat builder," said Taney, "that your sister and that African woman saved the life of my wife. I'll not forget what your sister has done. I'll make sure no harm comes to her while she's indentured to the innkeeper. Now listen well. One master should not tell another how to treat a servant. I don't care how this boat builder treats you. I'll not interfere with Cosgrove and the way he runs his inn. But I have told him no harm should fall on your sister. And he knows better than to have me as his enemy."

With that, Taney turned away without another word.

Paul was surprised by Taney. Did Taney mean Rebecca was safe? Could he trust this man who seemed to care so little about others?

"I don't know what happened," said Matthew. "But your sister's earned Taney's protection. I know you worry about her, Paul. I think you can trust Taney to do as he promised. Now let's get this lumber into Taney's warehouse so we can sail back to South River."

For a moment, Paul stood still, recalling Taney's words and all that had just happened. Would Rebecca be safe? Deep inside, he had no answer to that question. But a faint hope now rested by his deepest fear. And with that small comfort, he walked to the first canoe and began to unload the lumber.

14

Freedom on South River

As soon as the year's corn, beans, and squash were planted, Matthew gathered his clothing for the journey to St. Mary's City. It was time for the meeting of the colony's Assembly of Burgesses. Matthew had been thinking about this trip and preparing for months. He'd purchased a new coat, boots, and trousers with some of the money from the canoes he'd sold in Battle Town. He'd spent many evenings with Captain Burdett learning how the Assembly worked to approve the laws for the colony. The first impressions he made this year in the Assembly would be important for his future. All of the burgesses were men of means. Many owned several thousand acres of land and had more than a dozen men working for them. Matthew was entering a world of money and power. He didn't want to appear among the colony's elite as a poor, ignorant boat builder.

On the day of his departure, Matthew took Paul to the boatyard. "You've learned a great deal about building our canoes. But you're not yet ready to carve out a canoe from one of these logs by yourself."

"Why not, sir?

"You've mastered the chisels, the drawing knife, the hatchet, and the saw. But you don't control the adze well enough to strip away the wood from the outer and inner sides of the craft. So concentrate on making more oars, masts, and poles for the sails."

"Yes, sir," said Paul, trying to hide his disappointment.

"I'll return in six weeks. We'll begin building this summer's canoes then. Taney wants me to build a large rowing canoe that can hold seven or eight hogsheads at a time. Such a craft would be wider than any pine tree we'll find here on the Chesapeake. I'll have to consider how to make such a canoe while I'm away in St. Mary's City. We'll have much to do when I return."

Paul was deeply disappointed by Matthew's judgment. He'd tried hard to master the heavy headed adze. He could make deep cuts with each swing, but he couldn't control the cuts well enough to carve the top section or the outer shape of the canoe. He knew that Matthew's judgment of his skills was right. Still, he was disappointed that he'd made only enough progress to carve more oars, masts, and poles for the sails.

For the first week after Matthew left for St. Mary's City, Paul spent his mornings working in the cornfields and afternoons in the boatyard. Following Matthew's directions, he started to carve out oars for the new canoes they'd produce when Matthew returned.

After six days, Paul finished the first set of oars. But when he went to the shed for more wood, he found his heart was not in the work. Over and over he kept thinking about Matthew's words about his skills. He knew they were true, but even their truth could not stop him from feeling disappointed. Suddenly working in the boatyard had little appeal.

For the next few days, Paul continued to go to the boatyard. But his heart wasn't in his work. Most of the time he just sat in the shed, thinking about Rebecca and his life on South River.

Then an idea came to him. Here he was on South River. Here he was with his master away for five more weeks. As long as he did his work with Mary in the cornfields each morning and produced oars and masts in the boatyard, he'd have the rest of the day to himself. It was his first taste of freedom since coming to Maryland. It might not last long. He must use it now.

The next morning, Paul rose early, raced through his chores and went to the cornfield with the first morning light. Working hard, he finished cutting all the grass and weeds growing up around the corn stalks by mid-morning. With his field work finished for the day, he explained to Mary that he had things to do in the boatyard and would go there before returning to the cabin for his midday meal.

Paul had a plan. Matthew had taken his sailing canoe to St. Mary's City.

But there was an old sailing canoe with a broken mast down by the water that Matthew no longer used. The sail was missing the rope loops for attaching it to the mast, and Matthew now used the sail cloth to cover lumber in the shed. But the old sail was still good. With a new mast and pole and some rope to tie the old sail to the mast, Paul was sure he could launch the old canoe again and practice sailing on the river while Matthew was away. He'd carve a new mast and a pole for a sail. He knew he had to produce enough oars, masts, and poles over the next month to satisfy Matthew when he returned. But by working hard in the morning and half the afternoon, he could be free, sailing on the river for two or three hours each day.

First, Paul thought, I better examine the old canoe. Soon he discovered that he had to make some repairs. The handle for the rudder was broken. So he carved a new handle and fixed it to the old rudder with a set of oak pegs. Then he replaced the wooden pegs that held the oars in place for rowing. Finally he carried down from the shed a new mast and a new pole that would secure the bottom of the sail.

Ten days after Matthew had departed, Paul was ready to launch the old sailing canoe. It looked good with the new mast and the new pole at the base of the sail.

With everything ready, Paul placed his two oars in the bottom of the canoe and pushed it away from the shore. He rowed about 100 feet out into the river. There was a light breeze coming in from the Bay. After turning the bow into the wind, Paul pulled in his oars, placed them in the bottom of the canoe, put the rudder into its peg on the stern, and moved forward to raise the sail.

When he got to the mast, the wind had pushed the bow to the left and the breeze was now coming against his right shoulder. Paul pulled on the rope that ran to the top of the mast and back down to the top of the sail. As the sail rose up the mast, the breeze filled the cloth and caused the open end of the sail to pivot away from the stern.

The rope Paul needed to hold to control the sail was now in the water beyond his reach. His first thought was to lower the sail. But he realized if he did that, he'd drop most of the sail into the river.

Paul moved carefully back to the stern. He picked up his oars and placed them between the guide pegs that held them on the gunnels. He pulled on the right oar. The bow started to turn into the breeze. The sail's open end moved back toward him. When it was just over the left side, Paul grabbed the rope.

Once again the breeze began to fill the sail. He brought both oars back inside the canoe and caught hold of the rudder. Now he was ready to sail.

Paul felt the power of the breeze as the sail pulled against the rope in his hand. He'd done it! He was sailing. When he held the rudder just right and pulled the sail in close to the canoe, he could feel the craft increase its speed. When he let out rope, the sail moved away and the canoe slowed down.

Paul thought back to sailing with Matthew and what his master would do to change direction as he sailed down the river. Through trial and error, he let the canoe teach him how to maneuver, to pick up speed and slow down, to turn in a circle, and to almost stop by pointing the bow directly into the wind.

By the end of the day, Paul knew his plan would work. He'd do all his chores, work in the fields and the boatyard and still sail each day. He'd travel up and down South River. He might even sail out into the Bay. He would be obeying his master, doing his work, and still enjoying his first taste of freedom.

15

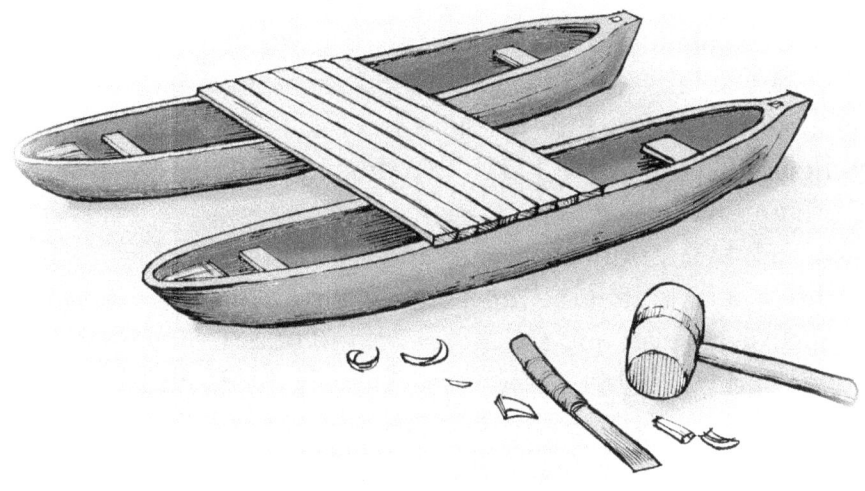

Building a New Craft

Each day Paul rushed through his work, eager to sail on the river. If he worked without stopping, he was ready to sail by early afternoon.

At first he stayed within sight of Matthew's boatyard. He felt safe close to the shore. He'd think about how Matthew handled the sail and rudder; then he'd try to control the craft in the same way. As his confidence grew, he went further out into the river and eventually, down into the Bay. After two weeks, Paul felt he was the master of his craft. With the summer days fast approaching and the light lasting longer each day, Paul stayed out on the river racing against the birds flying overhead and feeling the excitement of his new found freedom.

As he grew more comfortable on the water, Paul discovered a new experience. For the first time since coming to Maryland, his mind was free to wander as the canoe glided across the waters. He no longer had to concentrate on controlling the sail and adjusting the rudder. His hands seemed to move by themselves as he felt a shift in the wind or the currents in the river. He could look at the clouds, watch birds overhead, or listen to the water hitting against the canoe.

One afternoon he was thinking about all he'd learned from Matthew, about working with tools, about sailing on the Bay, about gathering the great pine logs and oak planks together into a raft and bringing them back from the Severn, when suddenly he heard Matthew's last words in his head.

Michael Taney wanted a canoe large enough to carry six or seven hogsheads of tobacco from his plantations to his warehouse on Battle Creek. But no tree on the Chesapeake was large enough for carving such a canoe. So why not use Matthew's method for building rafts to create the craft Taney had described?

Six to eight oak planks connected to two pine logs would create a platform large enough to carry those hogsheads. If the logs were carved into canoes long enough to support the planks and still have places for rowing, then you wouldn't have to pull the raft with a sailing canoe.

Paul could close his eyes and see this new kind of raft. He knew he and Matthew could build it. Could he convince Matthew it was possible?

The next day, Paul decided to test his idea. Instead of sailing, he'd build the new type of raft he'd envisioned. He had all the tools and the wood he'd need. Since he could not carve two full-sized canoes on his own, he'd create miniature canoes with his hatchet, chisels, and drawing knife. There were enough small pieces of oak and maple around the shed to use without destroying any of the larger pieces they'd need when Matthew returned.

Paul decided to make the two miniature canoes three feet long to show what this craft might look like when built out of thirty-foot logs. He found two pieces of maple in the shed that were long enough. All he had to do was to cut them to their proper size with a saw.

Since the maple timbers were square, he didn't have to use an adze to shape the top of these miniature canoes. Using his chisels and a mallet, he began to carve out the keel as Matthew had shown him. With the keel finished, he used his hatchet to cut away most of the extra wood from the outside and then shaped its final lines with his chisels. When he had the right outside lines, he smoothed out the outer shape with his drawing knife.

Now he was ready to carve out the canoe's interior. Again using his chisels and mallet, he carefully cut way strips of wood from the canoe's inside and bottom. Since no one would sit in the tiny canoes, he didn't have to worry about getting the right width to the walls or depth to the bottom. He just cut away enough wood to make each canoe look like the crafts they produced in the boatyard.

Even working quickly, it took four days to carve out each of the two miniature canoes. With them done, Paul turned to building the tiny oak planks that would connect the two canoes together and form the carrying surface of the raft.

First he cut a foot-long piece of oak from one of the discarded pieces lying in the shed. Then with his hatchet and a mallet, he split off one-inch strips along the length of the oak piece. In a few minutes, he had eight strips of oak, each measuring one foot in length.

Next he took his awl and drilled a small hole at each end of the oak strips. Then he drilled sixteen holes one inch apart on the tiny gunnels of his miniature canoes. Using a soft piece of pine, Paul carved out sixteen little pegs just wide enough to fit into the holes he'd drilled into the oak strips and canoe gunnels.

Paul picked up the first one-inch strip of oak, placed an end on one of the gunnels and pushed a pine peg into the hole. With a second peg he attached the other end of the oak strip to the outer wall of the other canoe. He continued attaching the oak strips until all eight were resting across the gunnels in the middle of the two miniature canoes.

Paul stepped back and looked at this work. At full size there would be enough room in each canoe for a man to sit and row in the bow and the stern. Two strong men could control the full-sized craft by rowing from the stern positions. With a full load of six or seven hogsheads of tobacco, they could move the craft down river with the help of the current. If the tobacco had to be sent up the river, four rowers might be required.

Paul was pleased with his work. Now he had something to show Matthew when he returned from St. Mary's City. The models were a good way to explain what he'd seen in his mind that day on the river. Now he was ready to go back to his work and wait for Matthew. But first he lifted off the eight oak strips from the two tiny canoes, placed four strips inside each canoe and carried the two miniatures to the back of the shed. He'd keep them there, safe and out of the way, until Matthew returned.

16

Michael Taney's Barge

Paul was finishing the day's work in the boatyard when he heard someone call his name. "Paul, come here to help secure the canoe and carry my things back to the cabin." It was Matthew. He'd returned from St. Mary's City.

Paul dropped his tools and hurried to the river's edge. Matthew was standing there looking at the old sailing canoe. Paul had forgotten about it and left the new mast and old sail in place.

"I suspect you've some things to tell me about this old canoe," said Matthew with an edge in his voice. "But that can wait. I'm eager to see my family after these many weeks away. We'll have much to talk about after I've inspected your summer's work and we start again in the boatyard. I've spoken to many persons in St. Mary's City about the craft Taney wants us to build. The men who came from England remember a type of craft they called a barge. It was used throughout the country to ferry goods, livestock, and people. By their descriptions, it was two or three times as wide as any canoe we can carve from even the largest pines here on the Chesapeake. But more about this problem another day."

As they walked past the boatyard toward the cabin, Matthew looked at the stack of oars, masts, and sail poles Paul had produced over the prior six weeks. "I see you've been busy. I was right to limit your work to those things you can produce without me. Now we can concentrate on carving enough canoes to make a September trip to Battle Creek worthwhile."

Paul wanted to stop Matthew and show him the miniature canoes and oak platform he'd created. He thought Matthew would be surprised when he showed him how they could build a craft similar to a barge. But he decided to say nothing. Matthew's steady strides toward the cabin showed him that their work could wait for another day.

That evening, to celebrate Matthew's return, Mary surpassed anything Paul had ever seen her cook. She made a delicious stew with salt pork, green corn, turnips, and something special she gathered at the edges of the cornfields called onions. She also brought in an armful of ears of corn wrapped in their leaves and roasted them in the coals in the fireplace. She fried oysters in a skillet and produced a pie filled with black berries gathered near the forest.

Paul and Matthew carried the family's table into the open area in front of the cabin door. When the sun finally set late that day, everyone was still drinking cider and enjoying the wonderful food. Little Martha was asleep in Mary's lap. Her baby brother was awake in his father's arms. Susan was singing softly by his side.

The next morning, Paul raced through his work in the cornfields to get back to the boatyard. When he arrived, Matthew surprised him. "Take my axe and your hatchet and follow me. We won't be working in the boatyard today. I've decided to mark more trees here and on the Severn for my tenants to cut this winter. I've new orders for canoes from members of the Assembly in St. Mary's City. I've decided to hire a man to work with us in the yard. "

"Why?"

"If I can secure enough pine, oak, and maple, I'll double our production. Today we'll mark and cut off the bark in a circle around some of the trees here on my lands. Tomorrow we'll sail to the Severn."

All day Paul followed Matthew through the forest. They had no trouble finding more maple and oak. When Matthew spotted a suitable tree, he'd mark it with his axe. Paul would follow and cut the bark in a strip about six inches wide around the entire circumference of the tree. By summer's end, the tree would be dead.

While Paul was killing the trees in this way, Matthew continued to look for suitable pines. He rejected every tall pine they found. "None is wide enough to build the type of barge Taney has ordered. I'm sure we'll find wider pine trees when we go to my land on the Severn."

But their search for the widest possible pine trees was no more successful on the Severn than on South River. Matthew finally marked half a dozen pines that were similar in size to the ones now waiting in the boatyard for their summer's work. He wasn't pleased. But he had to accept the best his land could produce.

On the sail back to South River, Matthew seemed defeated by their unsuccessful search. "I don't know how I'll construct this new type of craft Taney seeks. If I had one of those barges they build in England, I could take it apart and learn how to build it with the wood and tools we have here on the Chesapeake."

Paul could not remain quiet any longer. "Sir, I believe I know how we can build a type of craft that will do the work of one of those English barges."

Matthew cast a surprised look at Paul. If I don't know how to design a barge, he thought, how can this young boy do it? Finally, keeping a careful eye on Paul, Matthew asked: "What do you mean?"

Paul didn't hear the suspicion in Matthew's question. So he hurried on with his explanation, eager to share his invention with his master.

"We can use the pine logs and oak planks we already have in the boatyard to construct a raft similar to the ones we build when we bring lumber and logs back from the Severn."

"I can't sell a raft to Taney. You can't row a raft or control its journey down a river unless you're towing it behind a canoe. And there's no reason for Taney to pay me more than the value of the pine logs and oak planks if that's all I offer him."

"I understand," said Paul. "But I have a solution to show you. Wait until we get back to the boatyard. I don't have the right words to describe the craft we can build and sell. But when you see what I have in the shed, I know you'll understand what I mean."

Matthew was about to ask more questions, but remained silent for a few minutes. Had this young boy forgotten who was his master, he thought. Did I make a mistake leaving him to work alone while I was gone? Again he looked at Paul, trying to decide why he suddenly felt suspicious. Unable to find a reason, he decided he'd nothing to lose by giving Paul a chance to prove his words.

"Alright then, I'll wait until we reach the boatyard. In the meantime, tell me why I found a sail and new mast on the old canoe when I returned from St. Mary's City."

With pride in his voice, Paul explained how he'd decided to teach himself to sail by repairing the old canoe and carving a new mast and pole. He quickly added that he only sailed each day after finishing his work in the cornfields and boatyard, and had made sure to produce extra oars, masts, and poles while Matthew was away.

"Then take charge of the rudder and this sail," said Matthew, "and show me what you've learned. If you can bring us back to my boatyard safely, I'll judge your work and your learning most satisfactory."

One hour later, Paul brought the canoe to the shoreline by the boatyard. As he and Matthew pulled the craft higher up on the land, Paul thought he saw a smile on Matthew's face. "You've learned well. Now let's see this new raft you claim will work as a barge."

Paul ran ahead and retrieved his two miniature canoes with their tiny oak planks and the little pins to hold them in place. "I couldn't create a full-sized rowing raft and didn't want to spoil any of the pine logs and lumber we'll work with this summer. So I used small pieces of maple, oak, and pine that were left from other work. I've carved out two miniature canoes. With these pieces of oak and these pins, I'm able to build a platform between the two canoes."

"How will it work for Taney?" asked Matthew.

"The canoes will support the platform above the water and will have room for men to row in both the stern and the bow," said Paul. "If we build a craft such as this with thirty-foot pine logs and ten-foot oak planks, it should be able to carry at least six hogsheads down any river in the colony."

"A raft you can row," said Matthew. "When you first described it I didn't understand how it could work. I can tow a raft. But I can't row it. So the name you used didn't make any sense to me. Now I see that you've combined a raft with two canoes. Paul, I think you've found the solution I've been seeking. But we must find a new name for this craft."

"What about calling it a 'barge?'" Paul asked.

"They already use that name in England for a very different craft," Matthew replied. "We need a name that suits a craft built here in Maryland."

Matthew picked up Paul's model again, looking closely at its construction. For Paul, seconds began to feel like minutes and minutes like hours as he waited for Matthew to find the right name.

Finally a smile started to form on Matthew's face. "We'll call it our Chesapeake Bay barge. It may not be the same as the barges in England. But little about this colony seems to be like that old country. And planters up and down the Bay will know they are buying something made especially for them when they get our Chesapeake Bay barge."

"Now I can sell planters two rowing canoes instead of just one. With the oak planks and extra wooden pins to link them together, I can charge just as much for each rowing canoe as I charge for a sailing canoe. Tomorrow we'll start building our first Chesapeake Bay barge. We must test this new craft before we offer it to Taney. If it works, I'll want to build two of them to take to Battle Town this September. Since you can sail by yourself, we'll tow the rowing canoes behind our two sailing canoes and carry the oak planks for the platform in each rowing canoe."

With that, Matthew unexpectedly put his arm around Paul's shoulder. "Put your work back in the shed. I've seen enough for today. I don't think I want more surprises from you, at least not right away," Matthew said with a laugh. "Let's go back to the cabin and see what Mary's prepared for us to eat."

17

Back to Battle Creek

It was late September when Matthew and Paul sailed into Battle Creek with the four new canoes trailing behind them. Once again the shoreline showed the coming fall colors, with the maple leaves turning bright reds and yellows against the deep greens of the pine trees and the beeches taking on their dark copper hue. Paul was surprised at how much he welcomed the sight of Battle Town. Even with all of the hard memories it brought to mind, this place was important in his life. Rebecca was here. Matthew's business was here. On this trip they'd sell a new type of craft he'd designed, and with that proud feeling, Paul followed Matthew up into the bright, shining waters of Battle Creek.

Matthew was the first to reach the wharf. He still handled his sailing canoe better than Paul. He dropped the sail easily and rapidly rowed the final 100 feet to the wharf without any problems.

As Paul approached the wharf, he gradually turned his sailing canoe into the wind in order to lower the sail, carefully moving to the bow and mast. On his first attempt, his canoe slipped sideways to the wind and the sail swung out over the water. Paul quickly worked his way back to the stern, adjusted the rudder and turned the canoe back into the wind. With the sail hanging loosely over the side, Paul moved forward and untied the rope holding it at the top of the mast. Moving back to the stern, he lifted the oars from the bottom of the canoe, inserted them between the guide pegs, and rowed to the wharf. Practice, he thought. I still need to practice if some day I'm to sail as well as Matthew.

Matthew already had tied his canoe to the wharf and pulled the two canoes he'd been towing over to the shoreline to the left. "Pull your two next to mine as soon as you've secured your sailing canoe to the wharf. I'm going to find Taney and bring him here so we can show him the new Chesapeake Bay barge we've created."

When the canoes he'd been towing were safely next to Matthew's, Paul began to lift out the ten-foot oak planks. He wanted to get one of their barges put together before Matthew returned with Taney. He knew their success was important. The barges had to look their best if Taney was to buy them.

After working on the new Chesapeake Bay barges all summer and testing them on South River, Paul thought he could secure the planks across the two canoes with his eyes closed. Lifting the heavy planks was the hardest part. Once he got them sitting on the gunnels, it was easy to secure them in place by pounding the wooden pegs through the holes in the planks.

Matthew had made some changes in Paul's original design. He decided each plank should have two holes drilled into each end. That meant Paul had to drill twenty holes into the gunnels of each canoe. The extra pegs made the planks more secure and made the barge more rigid. Matthew had also left the sidewalls of these canoes thicker than a sailing canoe so that they would not crack under the stress of holding the planks in place.

Paul was setting the last plank down when he heard Matthew approaching with Taney. "We call this new craft a Chesapeake Bay barge. As you can see, we built it out of two rowing canoes that are strong enough to support an oak platform. There are rowing positions for four men. But you only need two to control the barge if you are bringing hogsheads down the Patuxent to Battle Creek.

"After your rowers deliver the tobacco to your warehouse, they can remove the oak platform and row back up the river in two separate canoes, carrying the planks and securing pins with them. If a planter has to bring his tobacco upriver, then he'll need four men to row the barge. In either case, the buyer gets two strong rowing canoes that can be converted into a larger barge when needed to carry six or more hogsheads to a warehouse or out to a ship."

"Have you tested these barges?" asked Taney. "How do I know they'll work?"

"We've tested them on the South River. I already have planters there who want to purchase them. But I told them they'd have to wait until I delivered these first two barges to you. You were the person who proposed the idea of a craft that could carry more than three hogsheads at a time. I feel obligated to give you the opportunity to purchase the first Chesapeake Bay barges built in the colony. I give you my word they'll do everything I've said. If they do not, then next spring when I return to Battle Town I'll give you back your money."

"That's a fair offer, and your price is fair too. I'll take both barges, and if you want, I'll take orders for others on the same terms we agreed to when I sold your other canoes. Come back with me to my warehouse so we can complete the purchase. "

"Paul," said Matthew, "leave the canoes and come along to Mister Taney's warehouse. You may purchase twenty shillings of clothes from his stores from the monies he's paying for the barges."

"You're too generous a master," said Taney sharply with a disapproving frown. "Why do you spoil this servant?"

"The design for these barges was his idea. He's becoming a very fine boat builder and a contributor to the success of my enterprise. Fortune was good to me the day you told Captain Darby you didn't want this boy. For me he's worth three times what I'll pay for his indenture."

Taney didn't say anything in reply, but looked at Matthew closely with a harsh scowl. Was this boat builder mocking him? Was he suggesting he'd gotten the better of Michael Taney, who purchased a troublesome criminal instead of this young boy who was showing such promise? But Matthew's face showed no sign of contempt or malice. Finally Taney decided that Matthew had meant no insult by his words. And when it comes to purchasing these castoffs from England, no man can know if he has purchased a prize or a scoundrel.

In any case, branding McNeely had produced positive results. The young man had started to obey his overseer and win his good judgment. He was using his anger and strength to make other servants work harder and obey the overseer. In the end, the Taney plantations would benefit from his service.

By this time, Paul had caught up with both men, but was walking behind them out of respect. As a servant, he knew he should not act as if he were their equal. With Matthew, he now could speak his mind and work without fear. But when Matthew was conducting business with men like Taney, Paul knew to stay in his place.

Besides, he was busy thinking about what he'd buy with the twenty shillings. By the time he entered Taney's warehouse, he'd made up his mind. He'd buy a new dress, a coat, and shoes for Rebecca. If he had any money after that, he'd purchase new trousers for himself. Other than trousers, he needed little. Matthew provided all he required. Buying these gifts for Rebecca would make for a wonderful surprise when he went to the inn to see her.

18

Confrontation at the Inn

Paul was surprised when he entered Taney's warehouse. From the outside, it didn't seem very large. But inside, every place he looked was filled with heavy iron tools or wooden casks or racks of clothing and shelves piled high with hats, buckets, ropes, cloth, and small cooking items. The big double doors in the front let light into every corner of the warehouse. So it didn't take long for Paul to find a good dress, a warm coat, and some shoes for Rebecca.

Taney had many items for sale, but the material for the dresses was all the same and the coats were different only in the thickness of the fabric. Even all the shoes were the same, except for the different sizes for men and women. When Paul added a pair of shoes to his other purchases, the total was nineteen shillings and eight pence.

He was pleased with his choices, and proud he'd earned the respect and trust of his master. At last, he thought, I can do something special for Rebecca. And perhaps Matthew will buy me the trousers when we return in the spring.

Matthew was still conducting his business with Taney when Paul finished buying Rebecca's gifts. "Go on," said Matthew. "I'll join you at the Punch later."

Paul didn't need any encouragement. He was eager to see his sister again and to give her the presents. As he walked toward the inn, Paul wondered how Rebecca's life had been under Cosgrove since he'd seen her last. Was it fair that his life with Matthew was going so well while she had to work for such a harsh master? What would he say if Rebecca asked him to take her away from the inn and back to South River?

He decided he'd not make the mistake of telling Rebecca all of the things that had happened since his last visit. It would be better just to give her the gifts and then wait to hear what she had to say about her life in the inn. With that resolve, Paul entered the Punch's main room. Fortunately it was late in the day. The room was empty. With luck he would have an hour with Rebecca before guests would demand their evening meals.

At that moment, Rebecca came into the room through the inn's rear door. When she saw her brother, she rushed over to him. "Paul, oh Paul, it's so wonderful to see you. I've missed you so much over these past months. I knew in my heart you'd be back. That helped me even when my life was hard."

Rebecca didn't pause for breath. The words poured out at such a pace she didn't even notice the clothing Paul held in his arms. Finally she stopped and looked at her brother. Paul could see small tears forming in her eyes.

"Let's sit here and talk," said Paul. "And here, these clothes and shoes are for you. My master has been generous because I've helped him so much in his boatyard. He let me purchase these things for you from Taney's warehouse."

Slowly Rebecca brushed away her tears and reached out to touch the dress and the coat. She took them from Paul and held them close to her chest. "Thank you, Paul," she said in a quiet voice. "My old coat is worn and no longer fits. Although I'm seldom allowed away from the inn, last winter was cold and there's little warmth where I sleep. I don't know if my master will buy me a new coat or any of the things I need. I must thank your master when I see him."

With the change in his sister's mood, Paul felt he could risk sharing his good fortune with her. "Rebecca, let's walk to the wharf while we still have some time. I want to show you the new crafts Matthew and I have built this year."

"My master will be angry if I leave the inn."

"We'll not be long. I want you to see our new barges. These craft don't yet exist any place else on the Chesapeake. They'll make Matthew known all around the Bay."

Rebecca looked at her brother and saw the excitement in his face. "Alright, but we must be quick. If you promise we'll come right back, I'll go. Let me take these clothes and the shoes to the shed where I work with Mama

Ailsworth. She's kind to me and will let me go if I come right back."

When she returned, she took Paul's hand and walked quickly out of the inn. But before they were half way to the wharf, Rebecca stopped and started to tremble. "I see my master down at the wharf with Michael Taney. We must get back to the inn before he sees me." And with that she dropped her brother's hand and ran back to the Punch.

When Paul caught up with her, Rebecca was still trembling inside the inn. "Come sit here with me," he said, "and tell me why you're so afraid."

Rebecca sat down at the table but said nothing. Paul waited. Finally she seemed to regain her calm and started to talk. "My master isn't like your master. If I anger him he takes a willow switch and hits me on my arms or legs. When the inn is full, I have to run between the cooking shed and this room to bring his customers their food and drink. If a customer complains that his food is cold or his tankard is empty, I'll get hit. My master seems to take pleasure in my pain. Sometimes he'll beat me with the willow when I've done nothing to earn it."

Paul reached out his hand to touch his sister's arm. Now come the tears, he thought, as he watched Rebecca start to tremble as she poured her sorrow out to him. He was surprised when she stopped and just looked into his eyes. Finally she seemed to regain her voice.

"I keep thinking about how they placed that brand on Timothy McNeely. Some day I fear that my master will bring charges against me and have them burn a brand into my flesh."

"Your master has no right to beat you or brand you!" It was Matthew. He'd come into the inn and was listening silently to Rebecca's tale. "The laws of our colony are strict when it comes to the service an indentured man or woman owes to the master. But the servant has rights to be treated well as long as he does the work the master requires."

"What are these rights of the servant that you describe?" asked Thomas Cosgrove, who had come into the inn while Matthew was talking.

"I talk about the right to fair treatment," replied Matthew, who turned to face the innkeeper. "You and I and every other landowner are bound by the laws of the colony to give our servants fair treatment. If what Rebecca says is true, then you're guilty of breaking those laws. So listen to my words carefully, innkeeper. Do not beat or abuse this girl. Her brother is my servant and I have an interest in his welfare and the welfare of his sister. When I return to Battle Town in the spring, I'll inquire about her treatment."

"Who are you to talk like this to me, boat builder?"

"Cosgrove, I'm not just a boat builder. I'm now a member of the colony's government. As a burgess in the Assembly, I'll not hesitate to bring charges against you in Lord Baltimore's Provincial Court if I learn that you've been beating this girl. And this day I've become a business partner to Michael Taney. It is he who will tell me how you have treated Rebecca."

Cosgrove looked at Matthew with anger in his eyes, but said nothing. He didn't believe this boat builder could cause him trouble with the Governor. But Taney was a different story. He couldn't risk angering Taney. For a moment, he searched for some way out of his dilemma. Then he turned to Rebecca. "Get back to the cooking shed, you lying, lazy girl. And as for you, boat builder, you're no longer welcome in my inn. No man tells me how to treat my servants. Now get, girl, if you know what's good for you."

Rebecca rose and fled from the room. Cosgrove turned, casting one last angry look at Matthew, and left the inn.

Paul looked with wonder at Matthew. "Thank you, sir."

"Don't thank me yet. My words may mean little to this man. We can't know how he'll treat your sister when we are on South River. I expect he'll continue to be harsh to her. But my words may stop him from beating her with his willow switch. If he beats her again, he'll learn that I mean what I've said and will see him before Lord Baltimore's court.

"Now let's leave this place," Matthew concluded. "I don't want to stay here any longer."

19

A Harsh Winter

Matthew's boatyard had never been busier. As soon as he and Paul returned from Battle Creek, they set to work building two Chesapeake Bay barges for planters on South River with the last logs harvested the prior year. Matthew was filled with confidence now that he had Taney ready to sell every new barge he could build.

As the days grew shorter and colder, he pushed ahead with an energy and enthusiasm that even surprised Paul. Matthew knew he might never reach the wealth and power that Taney possessed in Battle Town. But now that he could sell sailing canoes, rowing canoes, and these new barges, he was confident he'd build a prosperous future for himself and his growing family.

With the help of Jacob, the new laborer hired during the summer, the work progressed quickly. Paul's skills with the adze soon reached a level where Matthew trusted him to carve out the entire interior section of a canoe. Matthew and Jacob concentrated on carving the exterior shape and keel into each of the logs.

Paul enjoyed the new rhythm of the work. The hours passed quickly as he carved out each new canoe's interior, carefully shaping the seats, the gunnels, and the bow section where the future owner could mount a mast.

Now and then as he paused to examine his work, his thoughts reached out to Rebecca and her life in the inn. Was she safe? Was she well? Would Taney protect her? He didn't know, and that troubled him. But I can't do anything from here, he thought, as he turned back to his work.

By the end of December, four of these larger, heavier rowing canoes stood ready to receive the oak planks that would convert them into barges. Matthew was pleased with this progress. If they kept working at this pace, they'd produce two more barges by the time he and Paul made their spring trip to Battle Town.

Taney was sure to buy two more barges. Other South River planters had inquired about purchasing barges too. Matthew calculated he'd double his winter's income by producing the barges for Taney and still have orders to fill for local planters.

The only problem was they'd used Matthew's entire supply of logs. To build more barges, he'd have to sail to the Severn to bring back logs he'd ordered cut. It was a short sail to the Severn, but the harsh and unpredictable weather would make the journey difficult.

Matthew didn't have a choice. He needed the logs. If he watched the weather and waited for good winds, he knew that he could make the journey safely.

"Paul, tomorrow I'll take Jacob with me to my land on the Severn," Matthew announced as they sat over their evening meal. "I want you to stay here and work on carving more oars for our new barges. I may be gone for five or six days."

"Why so long?"

"We'll have to help my tenants move this year's pine harvest away from where they cut the trees and drag them down to the river. With the ground frozen, four of us should be able to drag the logs out of the forest over two or three days. It'll take another day to fashion them into a raft we can tow back here. If the weather's favorable, I'll return on the fifth or sixth day. If there's a storm, I'll wait till the sky's clear and the winds blow in our favor."

Paul was disappointed he'd not make the journey with Matthew. He'd never sailed on the Bay in winter. He knew it would take all of Matthew's skills to handle the rough waves and heavy winds. But he also knew he needed to stay with Mary and Susan. If a winter storm hit while Matthew was away, Paul would have to bring in extra wood and clear a way through the snow to the stream where the family drew its water. If the weather remained fair, he'd stay busy carving oars from the maple stock sitting in the yard's shed.

When Paul walked with Matthew and Jacob to the sailing canoe the next morning, the sky was clear and the winds were blowing steadily from the north. If these conditions held, it would be an easy sail to the Severn.

Soon Matthew and Jacob were out in the middle of South River moving rapidly toward the Bay. It's a good day, thought Matthew, and a good start to this journey. Sailing this time of year with the air cold and crisp adds something special to this trip. I've sailed to the Severn more times than I can count, he mused, but seldom has the journey been this good or important. If this weather holds, we'll be back before Paul has produced four oars.

It was just past midday when Matthew and Jacob pulled the sailing canoe out of the water and up on his land on the Severn. "Let's hurry, Jacob. We may not have enough light to pull the first log back here before this day ends, but at least we can clear the path through the forest and get the first log ready for tomorrow's work."

Matthew found his two tenants making repairs to their homes. One had a ladder set to the front of his house and was repairing the roof with new cedar boards. The other was building a shed on the side of his house to give winter shelter to his livestock. Winter was the only time when the tenants could complete such tasks. As soon as the weather turned warm in the early spring, both men would start their new tobacco seedbeds and begin preparing their fields for planting corn and tobacco. They could work on their houses only after their food was safely stored for the winter and the tobacco leaves were hanging securely in the drying sheds.

Matthew told them he'd require their labor for the next two days to pull out the four logs they'd felled for him in the late fall. After confirming the location of the logs, he and Jacob set out with axes and other equipment they'd need for pulling the logs back to the river.

To reach the trees they needed, they had to make their way through almost two feet of snow that remained on the ground from earlier storms. Breaking the trail was a slow process. But Matthew knew the snow would make the work easier by the time they'd pulled out the first log. The log's weight would pack it down and create a slippery path over which they could pull the remaining logs more quickly. So he was eager to get the first log ready for the hard work of the next morning.

Matthew carried two iron hooks he'd use to move the felled trees. Each hook was about eighteen inches long, shaped out of an iron rod one inch in diameter. One end was shaped into a sharp point that would go deep into the log. The other was curled into a circle about four inches wide. Matthew would drive these hooks into opposite sides of the pine log with his axe deep enough so the bottom of the circle almost touched the log's outer bark.

Jacob carried two coils of rope. After the iron hooks were driven into the log, he and Matthew would tie the ropes through the circular tops of the hooks. The other end of the ropes had large loops tied four feet apart. In the morning, Matthew and Jacob would take one of the ropes, slip the loops across their shoulders and harness themselves to the log. The tenants would do the same with the other rope and the four men, working together like a team of horses, would pull the log back to the river.

By the time they were finished setting up the first log for its journey, the light was beginning to fade. "At least we'll have warm shelter with my tenants and a good meal this evening. We'll need an early start in the morning if we're to drag two logs back to the river on our first day."

Three days later, Matthew had to admit his prediction had been wrong. Even with four strong men, the work had been slower and more difficult than he'd expected. The first log required almost an entire day before they reached the river. It was only after they pulled the second tree trunk from the forest that their trail was packed and smoothed enough to ease their labors. And when they reached the river with the fourth log, the wind was blowing hard from the south with storm clouds building in the sky.

The storm lasted two days, with fresh snow piling halfway up the sides of the houses as strong winds pushed it across the ground. Matthew and Jacob needed another day to link up the logs into a raft they could tow back to South River. Fortunately, when they were ready to sail, the sky was clear and the wind swung around to the north. If that direction held, they'd reach home by the middle of the day.

"May our luck hold," Matthew said to Jacob as they tied the final rope between the raft and their sailing canoe. "Securing these logs has been more work than I expected. We'll make the sail fairly easily if the winds stay steady from the north."

20

Pain and Sorrow

Matthew and Jacob were rowing up to the South River boatyard with the raft of new logs in tow when they saw Paul running toward them. "Matthew, come quickly. It's Susan! Mary says you must go to the cabin right away!"

"What's wrong?"

"I don't know. Susan was ill when I returned to the cabin after you sailed off to the Severn. She's not been able to leave her sleeping room since then. Mary has hardly left her side. Go quickly! I'll help Jacob!"

Matthew didn't hesitate. He ran to his cabin. When he entered, he found his daughter playing with her young brother in one corner of the room. Mary came down the stairs from Susan's sleeping room. "Go to her, Matthew," she said in a low whisper. "She may not recognize you, but stay with her. She's been fevered for the past six days. None of my healing mixtures have helped. For two days she's had trouble breathing. At times her eyes are open but she doesn't seem to see or hear me. I'll stay with the children until Paul returns."

Matthew rushed up the stairs. He was shocked when he saw his wife. Susan was pale. Her face was locked in struggle with some inner demon that would not let go. As he knelt beside her, he could see that she was fighting for every breath.

He reached for her hand. It was cold. After several minutes, Mary came to his side.

Matthew looked at his mother and whispered, "What can we do?"

"Nothing, except wait. I've done all I can, but nothing has helped. I fear for her. Many neighbors have asked for my help. Many are ill like Susan. Some have recovered. Others have died. This sickness is covering the land."

Matthew sat in silence. No one knew more than Mary about aiding the ill. Her words gave little hope. He looked toward his mother. "I've not seen you this tired since we waited those long days for Jose," he said softly. "Have you slept any while I was away?"

"Little. Even when others have come to the cabin to ask my aid, I've stayed with Susan. Paul also stayed here in the cabin. He's cared for the children while I've been with her, and when I've left her side to cook, he's sat with her in case she required help."

"Go and sleep. I'll stay with her now. I want to be here when she opens her eyes and to talk with her when she can hear me."

Mary looked at her son, hesitant to leave, but weary from long days and nights at Susan's side. Slowly she rose, placed a hand on Matthew's shoulder, and quietly left the room. Sitting in silence, Matthew continued to watch over Susan.

For the next three days they took their turns at Susan's side. Each day, Susan seemed to slip further and further away. Then she died.

Matthew and Mary descended to the great room below where Paul was watching the children. "Susan is dead," said Mary.

Matthew said nothing. He walked to the door and left the cabin.

Paul looked to Mary. "What should I do? Should I follow after Matthew?"

"Leave him be. He must learn to live with his pain and sorrow. What we need is a box of wood you English build as a place for your dead. Do you know this type of box?"

"Yes. My father called it a coffin. I watched him build one when my mother died. I have all the tools and wood I'll need in the boat yard."

"Then go and build this coffin. I'll stay here with the children until Matthew returns. Then I'll prepare Susan. We must hope Matthew finds in his children a way to heal his pain. But that will come only with time. When he returns he'll want to sit with Susan again. We must let him find his own way until it is time to place her in her box and remove her from this cabin."

Paul felt a sadness cover his heart. He wanted to say something to Mary. But what could he say? He wanted to go to Matthew. But he knew he should listen to Mary's words and stay away from his master. He looked at the children who continued to play in the corner. Mary turned to the fireplace to begin cooking again. With a heavy heart, Paul went to the boatyard to build Susan's coffin.

As he approached the shed where they kept the lumber and tools, Paul saw Matthew standing by the pine logs he'd towed from the Severn. Matthew looked at Paul, then turned and walked away.

Paul wanted to call to him, but said nothing. He knew what he had to do and how to do it. That helped.

It was dark when Matthew returned to the cabin. Mary offered him food. He just walked past the table and ascended the stairs to the sleeping rooms. Susan lay on their mattress. Matthew sat next to her still body. For the first time that day he could feel the water run from his eyes, down his face, and against the hand he held tight to his mouth.

Paul didn't see Matthew for the next two days. In the morning, Mary would bring the children down to the great room from her sleeping place where they stayed with her now that their mother was dead. Paul would eat his meal, then go to the shed to finish building the coffin.

He'd used his own body to set the dimensions for the box. He was taller than Susan and wider than she was in the shoulders. Using these measurements, he was sure the box would be large enough to hold her.

First he cut the planks for the bottom, sides, and top. Then he drilled holes along the edges of the bottom and side planks just large enough to allow him to drive in small wooden pegs that would hold the planks together. When he had the bottom planks connected to the four sides, he drilled small holes into the top edges and into the two planks that would form the top. The top would remain separate until they placed Susan's body inside. As Paul put away his tools, a memory of his mother's coffin flashed through his mind. Then his thoughts went back to his father, lost so suddenly in the storm. So many deaths, he thought. If only he and Rebecca could survive.

That evening Paul told Mary that the coffin was ready. "Good. It's time to remove the body from the cabin. I'll leave Matthew with his wife for this last night. Tomorrow he'll help you carry the box back here from the shed. Then we'll carry Susan's body outside and place it into the box. The ground's too hard to bury her deep enough so the foxes and wolves cannot get to her body. We'll leave the box in the shed next to the house where I store our corn and vegetables. Her body will soon be frozen like the ice on the streams. When that ice melts in the spring, it will be time to place her in the ground."

21

Spring on South River

The weeks following Susan's death were unsettling for Paul. Each day he'd rise and do his chores, then take his morning meal from Mary. At first he waited in the cabin for Matthew. When Matthew didn't come down from his sleeping room, Paul decided his place was in the boatyard with Jacob. Matthew, Paul reasoned, would come in his own time. So Paul put on his coat and woolen cap and hurried through the cold morning air to the boatyard. Now that only he and Jacob were working, there was more work to be done than he could finish each day. But the hard work quickly warmed his body and eased his mind. He was grateful for that.

Some days Matthew would come to the boatyard in the late morning and walk around the work. The first time Matthew appeared, Paul expected him to go to the shed, pick up his tools, and join them in the work. But Matthew just walked around the yard watching them. He said nothing. He did nothing. He just stared at them for a few minutes before walking away.

When Paul returned to the cabin for his midday meal, Matthew was nowhere to be seen. Paul ate his food and returned to the yard. He felt fortunate he and Jacob had work. Paul knew each step in the process. He could carve out the canoes without Matthew's help.

On the first log, when it was time to cut away the keel, Paul wished that he had Matthew's sure hands to guide him. Getting the keel right was the key to building a fine canoe. Paul took his time and used the wooden guide Matthew kept in the shed. Matthew could cut out the keel in a day. It took Paul two. When he was done, he stood at the end of the half-carved canoe and sighted his eye down the keel. It was as solid and true as any Matthew had made.

The first few weeks were hard for Mary too. She waited each day for her son to leave his sleeping room and join her with the children. Some days Matthew would appear late in the morning and immediately leave the cabin without saying anything to Mary or Martha or the baby. Other days he'd wait until Paul had left for the boatyard, then come down the stairs and sit silently at the table.

Matthew hardly ate any meals. He said nothing to his children. He didn't seem to notice them. If Mary looked into his eyes, Matthew would turn away and leave the cabin. After three weeks, Mary decided to speak. "Matthew," she said when he came down the stairs after Paul had left, "do you remember how it was after we lost Jose?"

"Yes, I remember. It was a difficult time. I wasn't much older than Paul is today. I knew how to build boats and how to sail my canoe. But that was all. We had our lands and the tenants to farm them. But Jose had managed all of those matters. He'd provided for us. I didn't know what to do."

"And I had to live without my husband," said Mary. "I had to live without the man who'd purchased my freedom from the Susquehannock and had provided for me and my son. And I had to show that son, who'd grown up but not yet become a man, what he must do as the new head of this family. Matthew, I'd little time to grieve. My heart was heavy then, as your heart is now, and I wanted to do nothing but feed my sadness.

"Our lives are filled with losses, Matthew, and also filled with gifts. You're my gift, as are these children. When we suffer a loss, as we have just suffered with Susan's death, we must learn to grieve without losing our gifts. It's your turn to learn this lesson. It's time for you to start living again, to care for these children, to return to your work. It's time for you to take responsibility for this family.

"Go out today, if you must, and spend this last day alone, saying goodbye to your Susan. But when you return this evening, be prepared to return as my son, as their father, as the man responsible for this family. Come back to us this way, or leave forever. Our lives must go on. I'll not see these children suffer any more by living with a father who neglects them."

Matthew stared at his mother. She'd never spoken to him this way. He felt dead inside. But in a corner of his mind, he knew she was right. He rose and walked out of the cabin.

Later that day Matthew appeared in the boatyard. Paul looked up briefly and then went back to his work. He was surprised when Matthew walked over to the canoe now sitting upright with blocks against its outer walls and keel. "You've carved fine lines for the outer sides of this canoe. The keel looks solid. The sides are smooth. She'll look good cutting through the water."

Paul kept working.

"We've a great deal of work to do if we're going to have two barges built by the time we sail to Battle Creek. Paul, tomorrow you'll continue to carve out the interior of this canoe. Jacob, you'll start the second log with me. Come here early. There's much to be done."

With that, Matthew turned from the work and walked back to the cabin. He wanted to hold his son and talk with his daughter. Tonight after their meal he'd put them to bed. Susan loved her children. He would find her again in them.

Paul knew there'd be many weeks before they were ready to sail to Battle Creek. There'd be many weeks before the snow was gone and the ground became soft enough to plant this year's corn and beans and squash. Before that planting, they'd find a place to dig deeply and place Susan and her box under the earth. As he walked back to the cabin that evening, he knew despite the dark clouds and cold winds that spring was coming. Winter was moving behind them. Matthew was with them again.

22

Returning to Battle Creek

S PRING 1674 — When the ground began to thaw and buds appeared on the apple trees, Paul knew the season was changing. It was time to prepare the fields for another year. Paul welcomed the change. He was beginning to enjoy the rhythm of the seasons in this new land.

The planting season was different without Susan. Mary remained in the cabin with the baby. Matthew took her place in the cornfields, working side by side with Paul to prepare the ground and plant the crops. Little Martha came along. Matthew told her that her job was to chase the birds. She'd remember from time to time, but mostly just followed after her father watching everything he did.

The routine in the boatyard also changed. While Paul and Matthew planted the corn and vegetables, Jacob began carving oars for the new barges. Once the planting was finished, Paul and Matthew would tend the new fields each morning. In the afternoons, all three men would turn to finishing the barges Matthew planned to take to Battle Creek.

When the barges were ready, Matthew and Paul loaded the four canoes with the oak planks and pegs for their carrying platforms, and added the 1,000 feet of planks they'd deliver to Captain Darby as Matthew's annual payment. Once again, Matthew would tow two of the new canoes behind his sailing canoe. Paul would tow the other two behind the old sailing canoe he'd repaired while Matthew was in St. Mary's City.

On the morning of their departure, Matthew told Jacob to tend the family's cornfields each morning and then work in the boatyard carving oars. They'd start work on new barges when he and Paul returned from Battle Creek.

As they rowed their canoes out into South River, Matthew thought about how different this year's journey would be. Jacob would tend their crops. Mary would care for Martha and the baby. Leaving them alone without his protection made him feel uneasy. His family seemed much smaller this year. It was smaller without Susan. What would I do, he thought, if I lost anyone else?

The challenge of towing the two barge canoes didn't give Matthew much time to ponder that question. As he rowed his line of canoes into the wind to set his sail, he noticed that Paul already was under sail and moving quickly down South River toward the Bay.

That boy is becoming quite a sailor, thought Matthew. Let's see how he handles his craft when we make the turn south out on the Bay. This day promises to bring us good winds for the sail to the Patuxent. I'll be surprised if he can reach the mouth of that river before me, even with the head start he's achieved this morning.

Without saying anything, Matthew decided to race Paul down the Bay. In the beginning, he was able to close the gap by pulling his sail in as close as possible to his canoe's gunnels and pointing the bow high into the oncoming breeze. He was less than 200 yards behind when Paul turned his head and caught sight of Matthew closing in on Paul's string of canoes. Suddenly Paul pulled his sail close to the side of his canoe and pointed his bow higher into the breeze. That's it, thought Matthew. You know we're racing. Now let's have some fun.

Paul was a better sailor than Matthew had anticipated. All the way down the Bay, Paul stayed just ahead. Even when the wind shifted to a new direction, Paul adjusted the angle of his sail almost as quickly as Matthew. Matthew tried every trick he knew to gain extra speed. By the time they could see the mouth of the Patuxent opening up on the Bay, he'd closed the gap so that he was just one canoe length behind Paul. But he could not gain the lead.

Matthew set the course of his canoe so that he stayed between Paul and the shoreline. In this position, he and Paul sailed toward the mouth of the river. But instead of turning immediately up into the river, Matthew kept sailing down the Bay. He'd trapped Paul, who could not turn into the river without sailing his canoe into Matthew's craft. When they were almost beyond the river's mouth, Matthew turned suddenly into the river and watched Paul try to maneuver his canoe to follow him.

Paul couldn't make the turn without sailing directly into the far shore of the river. Instead he had to turn in the opposite direction, sail out into the Bay, and then swing around in a large circle until he was facing directly into the Patuxent. By the time he completed the circle, Matthew was almost a quarter mile ahead on the river.

Looking back at Paul, Matthew relaxed. Their race down the Bay had cleared his mind. When they reached the wharf at Battle Town, he'd congratulate Paul on his expert sailing. Had it been a real race, Paul would have won. He'd reached the mouth of the river just ahead of Matthew. Matthew hoped Paul had learned a useful lesson. Watch out for the unexpected.

Paul was smiling when he rowed to the wharf and tied his canoe next to Matthew's craft. "You have become a fine sailor," Matthew shouted. "Now let's get these barges assembled. I'm sure you want to see Rebecca, and I want to talk to Taney. You may see Captain Darby in the Punch; that looks like the *Providence* at anchor in the harbor."

23

A Surprise Journey

After leaving Paul to assemble the barges by the wharf, Matthew found Taney in his warehouse taking inventory of the goods the *Providence* had brought back from England. "Welcome, boat builder," said Taney. "What brings you to Battle Town?"

"I've come to pay Captain Darby this year's oak for my servant's indenture. I also want to learn whether you've been satisfied with the two Chesapeake Bay barges I sold you last fall. I promised to return your money if you were not satisfied. What say you about those barges?"

"Keep my money. I'm well satisfied. In fact, if you had another I'd purchase it today, and my brother-in-law, Baker Brooke, who owns thousands of acres on both sides of the Patuxent, wants to purchase one of your barges too!"

"I'm pleased. And you're in luck. I have a new barge for you down at the wharf, and one for Baker Brooke as well. Will you send word to him, or do you want to purchase both from me and settle with your brother-in-law later?"

"I'll take them both, and I'll pay you something extra if you promise to only sell these barges to me in this area. Your price is fair, and I can add something to your price for my efforts and still sell them with ease to other planters."

"Done! I have no interest in becoming a merchant in Battle Town. If you send me word about how many barges you want to purchase, I'll make as many as I can and deliver them to you in the fall and spring."

"Before you go," said Taney, "I want to talk about this year's meeting of the Governor's Assembly in St. Mary's City. Baker is a member of Lord Baltimore's Privy Council. He has been talking to our governor about a new way for us to make our payments to the Calverts each year.

"The Calverts are proposing a tax of two shillings for each hogshead of tobacco each planter ships out to England. The Privy Council stands ready to approve this proposal. But how will the Assembly vote? That question concerns Baker. He's worried that the burgesses will oppose this change because the Puritans and Anglicans so often stand against the Calvert family because they're Catholics.

"As a member of the Assembly, what do you say? Will you support the governor and the Privy Council?"

"I'll have to think on this proposal, and talk with my fellow planters on South River. For me, it will shift my taxes from the land I own to the incomes of my tenants who raise and sell the tobacco from my land."

"What do you care about your tenants' welfare? There're plenty of men now in the colony who lack land and would be willing to take their places. Any man who owns more than a thousand acres, or who has tenants farming his land, will be better served through this new tax. That's why the members of the Privy Council all favor this change."

"As I said, I'll consult with my neighbors. And this year I may not attend the meeting in St. Mary's City. I've lost my wife to sickness and do not want to hire another man to tend my cornfields. I'll be busy enough filling the orders I expect for these new barges. Perhaps we'll send someone else to St. Mary's City as our South River burgess."

With that, Matthew took his payments and set out toward the Punch, pondering Taney's words. As he approached the building, he saw Captain Darby coming up from the wharf. "Good captain, I have this year's payment of 1,000 feet of oak waiting for you down at the wharf."

"Fine! I'll need all of that lumber for a new venture I'm undertaking in partnership with Mister Taney. I'll be sailing soon for Barbados with a load of corn and wheat Taney has gathered from the plantations up and down the river. There's a big demand for more food to feed the slaves on Barbados. By the way, did young Paul travel here with you again this year?"

"Yes. I expect we'll find him inside the inn visiting with his sister. Why do you ask?"

"I'd like to purchase his services from you for the eight-week sail to Barbados and back. My ship's carpenter injured his hand on the voyage from England and he'll need an assistant to build out the new facilities I require for this voyage. If you send Paul with me, I'll free you from the final two payments you owe for his indenture. Given the value of good oak timbers, you'll gain from my offer, and I'll have the help I need for the journey."

Matthew thought for a moment. Being free from the payments would be to his advantage. Now that he was building and selling these new barges, he could use all of the oak his tenants cut each winter. Sending Paul away for eight weeks would slow down their production. But he had Jacob to help him and could make some progress with Paul away.

"I accept your offer, Captain Darby. Now let's go and tell Paul. Let me explain this plan to him. I can see advantages for him too if he makes this journey. Of course he'll go if I tell him he must. He's obedient. Over this past year, he's contributed a great deal to my boatyard. I'm sure his skills will increase even more by traveling with you."

When Matthew and Captain Darby entered the Punch, they saw Paul and Rebecca sitting at a table in the far corner of the main room. Matthew was relieved to see that Rebecca was not crying. In fact, there was a smile on her face, and she was so engaged in the conversation with her brother that neither Paul nor Rebecca saw the two men as they walked over to the table.

"Hello, Rebecca," said Matthew. "You're looking well. How have you been since our last visit? Are you fairing well under your master?"

"Oh, sir," said Rebecca, somewhat startled, "I've been well. Since you last spoke with my master, my life has been better. I've been telling Paul that my master no longer beats me. He still yells and complains about my work. But Mama Ailsworth tells me he complains about her too, and about his wife and his children. I'm learning to cook from Mama Ailsworth. And the clothes Paul provided last visit have kept me warm this winter."

"I'm glad to hear about your welfare." Matthew paused, turned, and indicated the man beside him. "Remember Captain Darby? Paul, he has made an offer that will be advantageous for both of us. Please, Captain, sit with us so that we can talk."

Paul looked at Matthew, and then at Captain Darby, but said nothing.

"Paul, Captain Darby has asked me to sell him your services for the next eight weeks so that you can travel with him on the *Providence* to Barbados and back here to Battle Town. He needs your skills to help his carpenter build new storage in the hold of his ship. By allowing you to go with Captain Darby,

I'll be forgiven any more payments to him for your indenture. That will be a great advantage for me."

"And what's the advantage for me?" asked Paul cautiously.

"I've taught you what I know about carving sailing canoes. And now you and I are building Chesapeake Bay barges. In the future, I expect that there will be a demand for even larger craft here on the Bay. By sailing with the *Providence* and working with the ship's carpenter, you'll learn how English sailing ships are built. You've already shown me that you learn quickly and are most observant. Perhaps what you learn about making wood joints and new ways of fastening lumber together will be of use to us in the future."

Paul thought for a moment about Matthew's words. There was truth to what he said. Even so, something didn't feel right. What was it?

"You've sailed with me before, Paul," added Captain Darby. "You know I'm fair with my men. And I promise you, Matthew, I'll watch over him on this journey.

"Paul, I realize the last time we sailed from Barbados to Battle Creek, it was a hard journey for you and Rebecca. But that storm and the wave that carried your father from the ship were events I've not seen before or after in many years at sea. What's more, this time of year the weather is fine between here and the island. You have little to fear aboard the *Providence*."

That's true, thought Paul. It's fear that holds me back. I can see the advantages my master has presented. Now that I'm older and have some experience in the boatyard, there's much I can learn as a carpenter's assistant on the *Providence*. What holds me back is the thought of my father.

Matthew saw the troubled look on Paul's face. After waiting several moments for Paul to speak, he knew he had to help Paul make up his mind.

"Paul, we've both lost fathers to the waters," said Matthew. "I understand your hesitance. But do you see me refusing to sail on the Bay? I'd not send you on this journey if your life was at risk."

Paul felt Matthew's word touch his fear. Turning to his master, he nodded his head. "I understand what you've said, sir. I know I should go on this journey, and I will. I've but one request. Purchase a book of empty pages and some writing pens from Taney's warehouse so that I can make drawings of the inside of the *Providence* while I'm on this journey. In this way I'll bring back more than what I remember and will have things to share when I return."

"Done," said Matthew. "We have an agreement, Captain. Now, good Rebecca, please bring us some food and drink so we can celebrate Paul's new journey. Your brother and I will spend this night aboard the *Providence*, if

Captain Darby will have us, and as I remember his warnings, your food here in the Punch is better than what is offered on his ship."

As Rebecca made her way to the cooking shed, Thomas Cosgrove entered the room. At first he started to cross the room toward Paul and Matthew. But then he caught sight of Captain Darby, and stopped where he stood. For several moments he cast an angry stare at Matthew. Then he walked away.

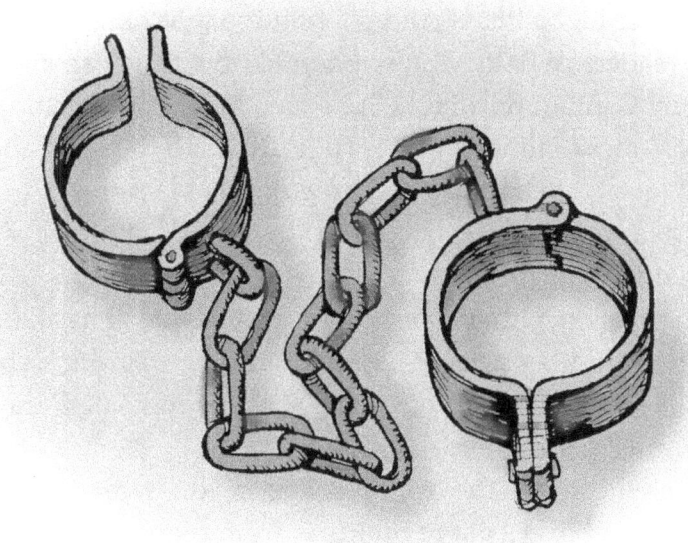

24

A Trial on South River

The corn in Matthew's fields was shoulder-high when Paul returned from his journey to Barbados. Summer's heat was on the land. The sun rose early and stayed above the western horizon until late each evening. Paul had missed the gentle days of spring. After all he'd seen and learned aboard the *Providence*, he was happy to come back to Matthew's cabin and the work in the boatyard.

For the first few days, Matthew tried to question Paul about the journey. All Paul would say was that Captain Darby had treated him well and was pleased with his work. Paul showed Matthew some of the sketches he had made of the *Providence*'s ribs, hull, and decking. But there was little from the drawings they could apply to their work in the boatyard. Beyond the drawings, Paul seemed reluctant to talk about the journey.

Matthew, Paul, and Jacob were working in the boatyard on two new canoes for their next barge when a stranger approached them. "I'm looking for Matthew DaSilva. My master, Captain Burdett, has sent me to summons Matthew to serve as one of the judges for a trial."

"I'm the man you're seeking," said Matthew. "What's the nature of this trial?"

"It concerns the blacksmith who came to South River last winter. The high sheriff from Battle Town, Michael Taney, has come here with charges against the blacksmith. My master calls you to serve as one of the judges. He asks you to come right away."

"Tell your master I'll be there. And tell him too that I know this man, Taney, who's one of the leaders in Battle Town. I don't know much about this new blacksmith. But tell Captain Burdett he'll be well served by listening to Taney."

Matthew took a few minutes to return his tools to the shed and then came back to Paul and Jacob. "What do you know of this blacksmith?" he asked Jacob. "You live near to where he has set up his shop. Is there any reason he should be charged with a crime?"

"I know of no reason. Others speak well of his work. His skills are needed in this area and his prices are fair. I'm told he pays his debts for the food he purchases and the small house and shop he rents near the wharf. I'm curious to learn how he's charged."

"I'd say come with me to the trial, but I need you here in the boatyard. We've orders for these barges we're building from planters on South River. And I've promised Taney I'll build barges for any orders he brings me. I expect to return with new orders when I see him at the trial. So stay working here. I'll tell you all the details when I return."

With that, Matthew turned and began walking toward Captain Burdett's house. It's unfortunate, he thought, that we don't have a place for trials as large as the main room at the Punch in Battle Creek. Captain Burdett has a fine home as befits the largest landowner in this area. But any trial brings many curious spectators. Usually there are more men who want to listen than could fit inside Burdett's home.

When he reached Burdett's house, Matthew saw his prediction was correct. There were more than a dozen men standing around the front door, which was open on this warm summer day. Matthew made his way through the crowd, which became easier when Captain Burdett called out, "Here comes Matthew DaSilva, the fifth and final judge we'll need to conduct the trial."

As Matthew took his seat at the long table where Captain Burdett and the other three judges sat facing the crowd, Burdett began the proceedings. "Gentlemen, we're gathered here today to hear charges of a crime brought against a new member of our community. I thank my fellow judges for joining me to deliberate on these matters. We serve to carry out the laws set forth by Lord Baltimore, as loyal members of his colony."

"Mister Taney, as High Sheriff of Battle Town, you bring charges against this man, Thomas Hagleton, who's resided with us in peace and prosperity for the last six months. What are the charges against him?"

Taney stood, resplendent in his expensive coat, pants and boots, and bowed to the judges. "Honored sirs, I charge him with theft of his master's property. This Thomas Hagleton is a slave who's run away from his master, Francis Perkins, who owns land on Battle Creek. I ask the court to turn this man over to me so that I can carry him back to Battle Town where he'll be punished as a runaway before he's returned to his master for whom he must work for the rest of his life."

At Taney's words, a somber expression came over Captain Burdett's face, and as he spoke, his voice showed his concern for the seriousness of the accusation. "Thomas Hagleton, how do you answer these charges?"

"I answer by saying I'm a free man who owes nothing to Francis Perkins. I admit I owed him five years of labor as his indentured servant. Perkins did pay the captain who carried me from Bristol to Battle Creek. But I worked my five years as a blacksmith for Perkins, who made a great deal of money by selling my services to this man, Michael Taney, and to other large planters up and down the Patuxent.

"Then, one year ago, my five years of service were completed. Perkins asked me to stay on his lands and to continue to work as the area's blacksmith. He told me he'd collect my fees from the other planters; and every six months he'd deduct my food and the rent for the blacksmith shop he'd built for me from the payments he received for my labors. He promised I'd receive the balance of the money as a free man working in partnership with him.

"I agreed to work in this way because it allowed me to save enough money to buy my own land and build my own blacksmith shop after a year of this arrangement. At the end of the first six months, I asked Perkins to pay me the money I'd earned through my labors. He protested that he owed me nothing.

"At first he claimed the payments he received only equaled the amount I owed him for my food and the rent of his blacksmith shop. But I showed him that I'd kept a record of every task I'd performed under our agreement, and that I knew how much money he'd collected from the other planters.

"When I showed him my records, he claimed he owned all the payments for my labors because I was his slave, as any planter on the river would recognize. I was amazed at his words. At first I didn't know what to do. That night, I decided I'd flee from his plantation and find a new place where I could start again as a free man. That's how I came to South River after walking north from Battle Creek for three days and three nights."

No sooner had Hagelton finished his reply, then Taney rose to his feet. "This man's lying to the court," he countered. "Look at him. You can see he's not English. He's not Irish. He's an African. No African comes to this land as an indentured servant. Francis Perkins told me he purchased this slave at a very high price because he'd been trained as a blacksmith. Perkins demands this man's service for all of his natural life. Only then will he earn a fair return on the monies he has paid for his slave."

The room was quiet after Taney finished. Captain Burdett looked first to the judges at his left. Then he turned to the judges on his right. No one spoke. "What do you have to say now?" he asked Hagleton.

"Mister Taney speaks the truth when he says I'm an African, but that is the only truth I'll recognize. I was born in Manchester. My father was an English sailor. My mother came from the West Coast of Africa, where my father met her when he was sailing on a Dutch vessel. He purchased her from her tribe and brought her back to England as his wife. When he died years later, my mother apprenticed me to a blacksmith, where I learned my trade.

"When I came of age, I signed on with a ship's captain to come to Maryland where I could practice my faith as a Catholic and where I was told I could earn my freedom and the chance to buy land of my own. As proof, I offer to the court my copy of the agreement I signed with that sea captain. Upon arrival in this colony, I was to be sold by him as an indentured servant for a period of five years." With that, Hagleton reached into his coat, pulled out a document and presented it to Captain Burdett.

"Any man can have a document written for him," claimed Taney. "Do you trust a piece of paper you've never seen before or the proof of your eyes? He even admits that he's an African. I ask you to recognize his status as a slave and his crime of running away from his owner. I ask the court to give him over to me to take back to his punishment and his owner."

For a moment, Matthew stared at Taney, who'd promised to sell his canoes to planters up and down the Patuxent. It would be so easy to do what he asked, thought Matthew. But was it right? He looked at Hagelton, a man he did not know. Then, looking into the man's face, he knew what he had to do.

"Wait," said Matthew. "We should not dismiss this man's words just by the way he looks or by his admission that his mother was an African. My fellow judges, please remember my father, Jose DaSilva, who came to this area as a free man and purchased his lands from Captain Burdett. Remember that he had a permit from Lord Baltimore to trade in beaver pelts, and that he was loyal to the Calverts and the government of this colony."

Matthew paused. Everyone was waiting for his next words. He knew what he had to do, but still he paused. Saying more was not easy or without danger.

"What you don't know," Matthew said slowly, "is my father also was… well… he was an African. His father was a Portuguese sailor who, like this man's father, married an African woman who was his mother. By birth to her, Jose was an African. But he came to this colony as a servant indentured to the Jesuit Fathers and served them for the five years. As an indentured servant, he was not a slave. What I am saying is that being an African does not make a man a slave. If what this man says about his document is true, then he too has earned his freedom."

"Boat builder," said Taney quickly, "are you standing against me and the planters of Battle Town? Are you denying that this man is a slave?"

Matthew paused again. He could feel Taney's eyes glaring at him. He sensed the silence in the room. Finally, he found his voice. "Please, Captain Burdett, let me see that paper."

Captain Burdett handed the paper to Matthew, who took only a moment to read it and then gave it to Michael Taney. "Mister Taney," Matthew said, "I see on this document the signature of Captain Amos Darby of the *Providence*, a man you and I both know well, who has been carrying men from England to serve as indentured servants in Battle Creek for many years. I recognize his signature because it's the same as what he wrote on the document I received from him when I purchased my servant, Paul, three years ago. I fear that this man, Francis Perkins, has lied to you and the citizens of Battle Town. From all that I can see, Thomas Hagleton has earned his freedom and owes no more service to Perkins."

Barely able to conceal the anger in his voice, Taney turned on Matthew. "Boat builder," he replied, glaring at Matthew before continuing to speak, "think carefully about your words. Will you stand witness for a slave against your fellow landowners, the men who buy your canoes and barges? Look again at that paper. Are you still sure the signature belongs to Darby?"

Matthew looked deeply into Taney's face before turning his eyes again to Hagelton's document. As he pretended to read it again, his mind went to the barges being built in his boatyard and to Taney's promise to buy all he could build. Was he mistaken about the signature? Should he ask the court for time to go to his home and get the indenture document Captain Darby had signed for Paul? Suddenly Matthew realized that Burdett's home was absolutely still. All eyes were turned to him. Everyone understood Taney's words and the threat he'd made.

Mathew looked at Taney, whose gaze was locked on his face. Matthew turned to Hagelton and then looked at Captain Burdett. Taney's face was easy to read. But Burdett gave no sign of what Matthew should do. What should he do?

Moments went by. Finally, Matthew found his voice.

"My fellow judges, I recommend we end this trial and find Thomas Hagleton free to pursue his life and work as he will here on South River or any place else in this colony."

"What," cried Taney, "will you be a traitor to your class?"

Paying no attention to Taney's outburst, Captain Burdett turned to the other judges. "Does anyone not agree with Matthew? Hearing no dissent, I rule that Thomas Hagleton is a free man. This ends the trial. With no disrespect to you, Mister Taney, we suggest you return to Battle Town."

"I'll return to my home," replied Taney. "But I'll not forget this act of injustice here on South River. The planters on the Patuxent will look to your decision as a theft of our property. Don't expect any sympathy or kindness from us should you have any business in the future before the court in Battle Creek."

With these final words, Taney looked directly at Matthew, who could feel the anger in his eyes. Then Taney turned and left Captain Burdett's home.

Matthew had little time to consider Taney's words. Thomas Hagleton had come forward and was shaking his hand and thanking him for the strength of his argument. Before Matthew could reply, Captain Burdett interrupted them both.

"Thomas Hagleton, as you've heard, we've found you a free man. As a judge, I'm pleased with our decision. As a plantation owner and member of Lord Baltimore's Privy Council, I must warn you that you've become an enemy of some powerful men. You may stay here if that pleases you. But I suggest you consider moving further north, away from any place where knowledge of your location may reach back to Battle Creek. I say these words not in malice, but only from experience. Heed them, or stay here at your own peril."

Taking Hagleton's arm, Matthew said in a low but gentle voice, "I hear much truth in Captain Burdett's words. Come sir. Walk with me to my home and boatyard. I too suggest you continue your travels north and go to the top of this Bay where there are few large plantations, and where many former indentured servants like yourself are finding they can purchase small sections of land. Your safety will be greater there, and with your skills as a blacksmith, you'll be welcome in any community where you choose to stay."

"But how will I get there?" asked Thomas. "It took most of my strength to make the three-day journey to South River when I fled Battle Creek. From what I know of this Bay, it could take me a week or more to walk to the area you've described. There'll be many dangers for a single man like me on such a journey."

"That's why I've asked you to come with me. In your story, I heard the voice of my father. He calls on me to help you. I build rowing canoes, and will offer you one with oars to make your journey north faster and safer. I've been told that you're an honest man who pays his debts. You can pay me for this canoe after you get settled in your new home, or you can send it back to me, which will close your debt. In either case, the canoe will carry you north in safety. What do you say to this offer?"

"What can I say, sir? You offer me a means to avoid both harm and vengeance. For that I owe you my deepest thanks. You've my word that I'll repay your kindness. I'll find some way to return the full value of your canoe."

25

Loss of Trade

The sun was touching the tall oaks to the west of the boatyard when Matthew and Thomas came back to where Paul and Jacob were working. Without stopping to talk to either man, Matthew walked with Thomas to the water's edge.

"This is my sailing canoe. It's a sturdy craft and easy to row. I'll remove the mast and sail since I can't take the time to teach you how to use them. But any man can row with a little practice. With your strength, it'll take no more than two days to reach the north of the Bay where I recommend you find your new home.

"Sit in the canoe with your face to the stern. Set the oars inside the set of pegs on top of the gunnels. The pegs hold the oars in place when you row. It takes some practice to steer in the proper direction when you're facing the stern, but in that position you can use the full strength of your arms, shoulders, and legs to pull the oars through the water. Practice for the remainder of this day and tie the canoe this evening to the wharf near your blacksmith shop. The canoe will carry you and your possessions safely as long as there's no great storm on the Bay."

"When you row out of South River tomorrow, turn to the north and follow the shoreline for the next two days. Soon you'll come to the mouth of another river, called the Severn. Continue rowing north. By the afternoon you'll reach a second river, called the Magathy. Row into this river.

"You'll find a small island there just a short distance from the Bay. That'll be a safe place to spend the night. No animals will bother you while you're on the island. The water's safe to drink and free of the salt you find in the rivers to the south.

"Continue rowing along the shoreline on your second day. By noon you should reach a place where a third river separates the shoreline into two parts. We call this river the Patapsco. When you reach it, you'll be near places you can explore for a new home. Cross over to the far shoreline. You'll see a long arm of land reaching out so far that it almost stretches across the river. Thomas Sparrow owns this land.

"My father, Jose DaSilva, knew Sparrow well and helped him establish peace with the peoples who hunted this area long before any English settled there. Sparrow is a good man and a friend. Tell him I've sent you to him. He'll give you shelter and can advise you where you might best settle and set up your blacksmith shop again.

"If you can't find Sparrow or want to go further, continue west on that north shoreline. Within an hour after leaving Sparrow's land, you'll find a wharf owned by William Fellson. He's also a friend and another who'll offer you shelter when you say I've sent you."

Thomas stood silently for a moment, listening carefully and absorbing all that Matthew had told him about his trip north in this strange craft. Finally, realizing that Matthew had finished his instructions, he smiled at his benefactor.

"Sir, I can only thank you now. But I'll never forget the aid you've offered me, and will repay it tenfold some day."

"Now you should get started," replied Matthew quickly. "You'll need the balance of this day to become comfortable with this canoe and gain confidence for your journey."

After removing the mast, the sail, and the rudder, Matthew helped Thomas launch the canoe. He watched Thomas struggle with the oars for a few minutes. Then, as Thomas began to control the canoe better, Matthew turned back to the boatyard and his work.

"Why have you given that man your best sailing canoe?" asked Paul.

"What happened at his trial?" added Jacob.

Matthew wanted to get back to his work. But he knew he'd only get more questions and no work from these men until he answered them. Matthew recounted the events in Captain Burdett's home. Like the men at the trial,

Paul and Jacob were surprised when Matthew talked about Jose's African heritage. When Matthew repeated Taney's warning at the end of the trial, he paused.

"I know from Taney's words I've lost all my business on Battle Creek and the entire Patuxent area this day. Taney was very angry with me for coming to the defense of this man. He'll not buy any more canoes or barges from me, and I am sure he'll tell all of the other planters not to purchase from me again. It will not take long for us to build enough barges to supply all of the planters here on South River. Given their hatred of my father, I don't expect any Puritans on the Severn will purchase from me either. So my success may soon end." Matthew paused, letting the meaning of his statement sink in for Paul and Jacob. Then with a determined look in his eye, he said, "Whatever happens, I don't regret what I've done."

"I know this loss weighs heavily on you," said Paul. "But after my journey with Captain Darby, I'm glad we'll not have anything to do with that man, Taney."

Paul's words caught Matthew's attention. "What do you mean?"

"The cargo we carried back on the *Providence* from Barbados was a hold full of Africans Taney had purchased on the island in return for the corn and wheat Darby carried when we left Battle Creek. My work with the ship's carpenter was building wooden racks in the hold for twenty men who were held there in chains. When we arrived in Battle Town, Taney kept the five strongest men as slaves to work on one of his plantations and sold the others in front of the Punch to planters in the area. That's why I could hardly talk about my journey. I felt I'd built prisons for these men on the *Providence* and contributed to their suffering. I feared that somehow you'd be drawn into this slave business with Taney."

"Now I understand why Taney said at today's trial that we'd stolen property from all of the planters on the Patuxent," replied Matthew. "They no longer want indentured men from England. They want to own those they purchase for life. I'll have nothing to do with men who trade in the lives of others."

26

The Deliverance

Paul finished his chores around the cabin, ate his morning meal, and headed off to the cornfield long before the summer sun appeared in the eastern sky. Most days he enjoyed these early morning hours as the only time he'd be alone. But this morning he couldn't free his mind from the past day as he hacked with his hoe at the weeds and grasses growing among the rows of corn. What did it mean that Matthew's father was an African, like the men Captain Darby carried in chains from Barbados? Matthew looked so much like Mary and not at all like Thomas Hagleton. What did it mean that Matthew would no longer be able to sell his canoes and barges in Battle Town? What would happen to Rebecca now that Taney hated Matthew? Is this the end of our work in the boatyard?

These questions and others continued to roll through Paul's mind as he approached the boatyard where Matthew and Jacob were already hard at work. "Paul," said Matthew, "you look like the weight of the world is on your shoulders. It's as if Michael Taney has become your enemy rather than mine." The truth of Matthew's words caught Paul by surprise. Had his life really changed?

"You're right, Matthew," replied Paul. "It is your business that's now at risk. My only real sorrow is that I'll not see my sister if we no longer travel to

Battle Town. What will happen to her? I keep thinking her master will return to his harsh ways and beat her again. Is there nothing I can do to protect her?"

Matthew paused from his work, stood quietly for a moment, and then walked over to Paul. "I admit you've reason to fear. Cosgrove is a harsh man. When he learns from Taney what I've done, he'll no longer fear me. You must hope Rebecca is stronger now and will be able to survive the remaining two and a half years of her indenture. When it ends, you'll be free to travel to Battle Town and bring her here to live with us."

Paul felt little comfort from Matthew's words. He was about to ask his master if there wasn't something they could do to aid Rebecca right away when a voice called to them from the shoreline. "Is this the boatyard of Matthew DaSilva?" asked a man standing in the bow of a rowing skiff approaching Matthew's land. "I'm Captain Henry Comfort. You can see my vessel, the *Deliverance,* anchored out in the middle of the river. Captain Burdett said I should seek out the boat builder, Matthew DaSilva."

Matthew cast a glance toward the middle of the river, then back.

"The hull of my ship is leaking just at the waterline. My carpenter says he can no longer stop the leaks with caulking because cursed sea worms have eaten through the wood. Planks must be replaced. If you, sir, are DaSilva, may I come on your land to speak with you?"

"I'm DaSilva. You're welcome to come up here so we can talk. But I must tell you I'm a simple builder of canoes for rowing and sailing on the Chesapeake. I'm not a shipwright and have no experience repairing large sailing ships like this one."

Captain Comfort stepped out of his skiff and waded through the shallow water to Matthew's land. "My ship's carpenter is skilled. He knows how to make these repairs, and would do so back in England where the shipyards make them all year round. He simply requires some skilled carpenters, a supply of solid black oak planking, and a way to bring the ship up out of the water so that he can remove the rotten planking and replace them with new wood."

Matthew glanced at the ship now at anchor just off his land, gauging its size and the scale of work Captain Comfort had described. Never before had he considered such a task, and he carefully considered how best to answer the captain's request.

"I'll gladly sell you the black oak you require. My men and I are skilled enough to give your carpenter the assistance he needs. And you're welcome to use my shoreline for these repairs. But I have no way of helping you lift a large vessel high enough out of the water to make them. I know of no place on this Bay where they can help you make such repairs. Still, if you choose to purchase my oak planks, I'll sell them. Perhaps you can take them somewhere else where such repairs are possible."

"I dare not sail the *Deliverance* any further. Anchored here in the calm river, my men can bail out the water and keep her afloat. Out on the ocean we'll not make a single day of sailing before my good ship will sink. I must find a way to make these repairs here, on your South River, or suffer the loss of all my wealth in this ship."

Paul moved next to Matthew. "Sir, I believe I know how these repairs may be possible here on your land. When I was on Barbados with Captain Darby, I watched how they make these types of repairs to ships on that island. I've drawn sketches of this method in the book you provided. I didn't show them to you because there seemed no need for such equipment for your boatyard. But I know we can build a structure that will support this great ship and allow for these repairs in safety."

"This lad speaks true," added Captain Comfort. "I too have seen this method of making deep repairs they use in Barbados. It's different from our system in England. But it does work as he says."

"Tell me, captain, did you gain this knowledge because you trade in slaves in Barbados?"

"No, sir. I promise you I detest trade in men's lives as much as you do by the tone of your words. I'm what others call a Quaker, or what we believers call a member of the Society of Friends. For us, each man and each woman is sacred and free because each of us carries the divine spirit within our hearts and minds. I only trade with my Quaker brethren who've settled in large numbers on the eastern shore of this Bay and now are coming to your area as well. We enjoy the freedom of belief the Calverts have established for this colony after suffering whippings, prison, and death for our beliefs at the hands of the Puritans in the northern colonies and Virginia."

"I know of you Quakers," said Matthew, "and know that you can be trusted to speak the truth even at the risk of your lives. Show us how we can make these repairs, Paul. If the good captain agrees with your plan, we'll set aside our work on these barges and offer Captain Comfort the lumber and assistance he requires."

"I'll pay you well for this aid," added Comfort. "In addition, my Quaker brothers and sisters have need for the sailing and rowing canoes you build in this yard. I'll carry to them word of your good service and help you sell all that you can build to my brethren."

Matthew looked at Paul with a smile on his face. "Run quickly to the cabin and bring your sketches from Barbados. I believe we may have more work than I thought possible at the end of yesterday's trial."

27

Repairing the Deliverance

Matthew was surprised by the simplicity of Paul's plan to bring Captain Comfort's ship ashore. It required a structure unlike anything he'd ever seen on the Chesapeake. But all they needed were the right oak trees and the tools they used everyday in the boatyard. If it worked the way Paul described, Captain Comfort's ship would simply float up on to his land and the South River would do most of the work.

First he and Paul went into his forest to locate and cut down three oak trees eighteen inches across and over forty feet high. Jacob followed with Matthew's ox and the equipment they'd need to pull the fallen trees out of the forest.

After Matthew and Paul cut away the branches along the length of each tree, Jacob set hooks deep into the trees and tied ropes through the iron circles at the top of the hooks. Tying the other ends of the ropes to the harness of the ox, Jacob used the mighty beast to drag the trees back to the boatyard.

With their saws, Matthew and Paul cut one of the trees into ten-foot sections. They set three of these sections on the ground in parallel lines and placed two long oak planks across the ends of the three logs. Using their awls and large oak pegs, they drilled holes through the planks and into the ends of the logs and then joined the logs and planks together with the large oak pegs.

When they were done, the logs and planks looked like two large squares linked together. This structure would be the basic frame that would support the ship.

While Matthew and Paul were building the frame, Jacob dragged the other two trees down to the water's edge. He pushed the narrow end of each tree out into the water and secured the wider end about ten feet from the water's edge. When he was done, the two trees ran in parallel lines, about eight feet apart, thirty feet out into the river.

To hold the trees in place, Jacob took the remaining section of the tree that Paul and Matthew had cut and cut it again into five-foot lengths. Using his axe, he split each of these five-foot logs down the center, and then split each half down the center again.

Working with a large mallet, Jacob hammered one of the five-foot oak stakes down into the ground on one side of a forty-foot tree that stretched into the river. He hammered a second stake into the ground on the opposite. He repeated this process with the remaining six stakes, placing four stakes against the sides of each tree. When he was done, he tested his work by trying to roll each tree away from the other. The eight stakes held the two trees fast in parallel lines running out into the river.

Paul and Matthew hitched the ox to the two oak squares they had created, and dragged this large frame over the ground and up on to the two trees that Jacob had set into the river. The three logs that formed the cross sections of the frame rested on top of the two forty-foot logs Jacob had secured with the oak stakes. The planks that formed the other sides of the squares ran parallel to the forty-foot logs.

The three men pushed the frame down the forty-foot logs and out into the river until the farthest end just began to float. Using ropes, Paul and Matthew tied the floating ends back down to the forty-foot logs that were supporting the frame in the water.

"Now," said Matthew, "we'll wait five days until the moon is full and the tide is highest on the river. The high tide will cover this oak frame with enough water to let Captain Comfort bring the *Deliverance* close into the shore and position the hull over the frame we've set in place. As the tide goes out, the ship will drop down until the keel comes to rest against our frame. When it does, we must be ready with other oak timbers to brace the ship's hull in place against the frame and support it in that position when the river recedes back to its usual depth. Does that sound right to you, Captain Comfort?"

"Yes, Matthew, that's how it's done on Barbados."

"But how will you bring your ship that close in to the shoreline and hold it in place when the tide runs out?" asked Jacob.

"We'll tow the ship in close to the boatyard with our rowing skiff," answered the captain. "I'll place the rest of my crew here on the shore. When the skiff reaches the water's edge, my crew will take the towing lines and pull the ship into place over the frame. Matthew, can you set a series of strong oak stakes in the ground along the water's edge? We'll use them to tie the ropes in place once we've positioned the ship over the frame. With the stakes, we'll easily hold the ship in place when the tide runs out."

"We'll set the stakes in place tomorrow. "

"Good. Good," said Captain Comfort.

Matthew turned away from the captain and slowly walked around the new device they had built to Paul's specifications. It's amazing, he thought, how this young man can design new things in his mind and make them take shape, as if by magic. Now, let's hope it works.

"If all goes as planned," Matthew said after returning to Captain Comfort's side, "your carpenter will have three weeks to make the necessary repairs to your hull before the next high tide returns to the river and floats the ship back off the frame. Can you delay your departure that long?"

"I'm grateful we'll be able to sail out to sea again in one month's time," answered Captain Comfort. "If you and your men had not come to my aid, the *Deliverance* might have rotted and sunk here on South River. Now I'll be able to return to England and continue my trade with the good people of this area."

"Your good fortune will be our good fortune, Captain. Now let's wait for the tide and be ready to put Paul's plan to the test."

28

A New Partnership

R epairing the *Deliverance* required all three weeks after Captain Comfort's
crew towed the ship onto the platform and the men braced the vessel
securely in place. Paul was relieved when the platform worked as he'd
predicted. He also was excited by the new work in the boatyard. He followed
every step of the ship's repair. As the ship's carpenter removed rotten sections
of the hull, he carefully observed how the wooden planks were secured to
the ship's frame, how they were notched to fit tightly together, and how the
carpenter used caulking to fill the seams when the new planks were in place.

After the first day, Paul brought the book he'd carried on the *Providence* to
the work site and filled it with new drawings. He constantly asked the ship's
carpenter questions and added notes to each of his drawings.

"Matthew," said Paul one day as they ate their midday meal, "I think
I know how we can build a new type of vessel for transporting goods and
people around the Bay."

"What do you have in mind."

"We can use the new platform we've built for the repairs to the
Deliverance, to build our own sailing boats on it. All we have to do is follow
the methods the ship's carpenter has taught me over the past few weeks."

"Why would we want to build a ship as large as the *Deliverance*?"

"We don't have to build anything that large. Do you remember when I had the idea for using canoes and oak planks to create our new barges? I didn't make a full-sized barge. Instead I created a miniature barge by reducing the size of each part. We can do the same thing with the *Deliverance* if I make careful measurements of each section that forms the hull. With those measurements, we can reduce the size of each section and produce a much smaller craft that will fit the scale for sailing on the Bay. With such a craft, it will be possible to use sail rather than oars, and that should allow the owner to travel anywhere across the Bay with a large cargo."

Matthew sat silently for a few minutes, considering Paul's plan. "I think there may be merit in what you propose. Let's present your plan to the ship's carpenter and Captain Comfort. They know how ships are built back in England. If they think we can succeed, there may be many ways we can profit from building these new craft."

Paul could not wait to get back to the boatyard. Matthew smiled as he watched this young man so full of new ideas hurry to finish his meal and get back to the *Deliverance*. "I'm not very hungry today," he said to Paul. "Are you ready to go back to work?" Paul was on his feet and ready to go almost before Matthew finished speaking. As they walked down to the boatyard, Matthew smiled again as Paul continued to explain his plan, adding details and new ideas faster than Matthew could follow.

"Paul," said Matthew, "when we get to the *Deliverance*, let me present your idea to Captain Comfort and the ship's carpenter. Both men are grateful to us for the aid we've given them. It'll be too easy for them to say that your idea has merit and to hold back criticisms or doubts.

"We want to hear those doubts and criticisms now, rather than discover difficulties with the plan only after we have started to build the new vessels you propose. Every new venture brings problems that you can't anticipate at the start. If we can learn about some of these problems from the carpenter and the captain before we begin, our work will be easier."

At first Paul wasn't pleased with Matthew's words. It was hard to restrain his enthusiasm for this plan. He'd thought of this new way to build boats. He'd done the measurements and made the sketches in his book. He'd thought about his new plan for more than a week and already had quietly tested most of his ideas with the ship's carpenter. But Matthew was his master. Perhaps his approach was best.

"Captain Comfort," said Matthew, as they approached the *Deliverance*, "this young lad is trying to make me believe that it's possible to build a smaller version of your good ship right here in my boatyard if we carefully follow the design of the *Deliverance*'s hull and reduce the size of each of its parts to a scale that's appropriate for the Bay. What say you to this idea?"

"I say you have a special talent in this young man," said the captain. "You tell me he first thought of the design for these craft you call a Chesapeake Bay barge. I heard him explain to you how we could do these repairs to the *Deliverance* by building this platform and placing it in the river. Now he describes what ship builders have been doing in England for more than 100 years.

"All ships are copies of earlier craft. There are few original ideas, just improvements that clever men devise as they perform their work over and over again. Your Chesapeake Bay barge may work well on a river, but I wouldn't want to try to take one across the Bay. With a smaller version of the *Deliverance*, you'll be able to sail up and down this Bay with ease and speed. And you'll be able to carry more cargo than you dare load on one of your barges. I think you'll be wise to follow his plan.

"In fact, if you successfully build such a sailing vessel for use on the Bay, I'd make you an offer to enter into business with me."

Matthew fixed his eyes on the captain, wondering what this man would propose. Did he think they needed his help to make the boatyard a success? Why would a sea captain want to go into business with a simple boat builder?

"It would save me a great deal of time and money," continued Captain Comfort, "if I could sail here to the South River each year and find a full cargo of tobacco waiting for me to load. Now I have to sail to several places on the Bay and wait for the planters to bring their hogsheads out to my ship. I have to pay my sailors, even when we sit idle at anchor. If you build some of these smaller sailing vessels, you could gather a full load of tobacco here on your land and I'd pay you for that work. I'll provide enough money to construct a wharf that reaches out into the river far enough so that I can bring the *Deliverance* right up to its end."

"If you build a warehouse to store the tobacco here on your land, I can unload the goods I carry here from England into your warehouse and you can load the tobacco you have gathered onto my ship. You can sell the cloth and tools I store in your warehouse. I'll sell the tobacco you have gathered back in England. What say you to my proposal?"

"I'd say you have two new partners," said Matthew.

"What do you mean by two new partners?" asked Comfort.

"I say two because as of this day I'm releasing Paul from his indenture.

He's brought me more profit from his ideas and hard work than any master has a right to expect from a servant. It would not be just for me to profit alone from his proposals and the opportunities they've created for me. Whatever I'll earn from this new partnership with you, a fair share will go to Paul as my partner. Do you agree?"

"Done!" replied the captain.

Paul looked at Matthew in wonder. He could not believe what he'd heard. He was free. He was Matthew's partner. He'd build the new craft he'd seen in his mind as he worked on the *Deliverance*. Was this a dream?

"Captain Comfort," added Matthew, "I too have been thinking about new opportunities while we have been working on the *Deliverance*. When Paul traveled to Barbados, the ship carried corn and grain grown here on the Chesapeake for sale on that island where there's a great demand for such food. We have a great demand for the sugar and molasses they produce on Barbados. In our new venture together, Paul and I could gather a fall harvest of corn and grain that you could carry to Barbados each year and return with sugar and molasses to South River. Then we'll sell the sugar and molasses while we gather a new load of tobacco for you each spring and have it ready for you to take back to England when you return from Barbados."

"Done, again," said Captain Comfort. "I see I've two ambitious new partners here on South River. If we can carry out all of these plans, there'll be profit for all."

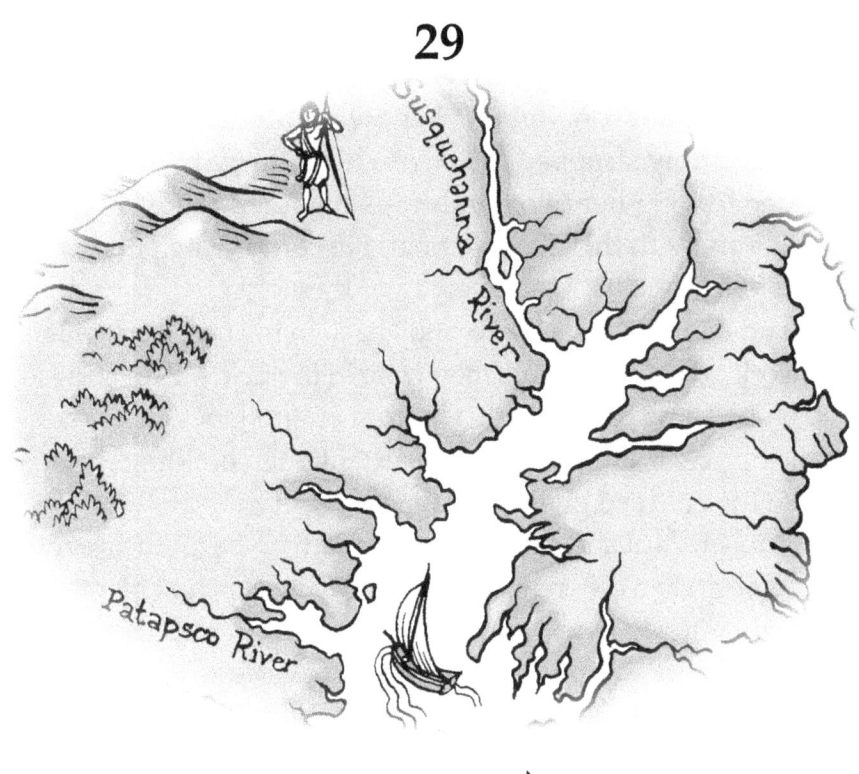

29

Sailing North

It was early September when Captain Comfort and the *Deliverance* finally sailed out of South River. The days were warm. The leaves were still green on the trees surrounding Matthew's cabin. The winds blowing off the Bay were gentle. But Matthew and Paul knew the season was changing once again. It was time to gather in the year's corn and squash. They had to get their household ready for the coming winter before they could start their new venture as merchant-traders in tobacco, corn, and grains.

Both men laughed as Martha struggled to help them gather the food. Martha had decided she liked best to pull the ears of corn from their stalks. But she was too short to reach any of the ears by herself. So she stayed right by her father's side as he walked along the rows of corn and pulled on his trousers until he'd bend a stalk down for Martha to grab hold of a single ear.

Matthew quickly realized he'd get little work done if he had to stop each time to allow Martha to pick off a single ear. But he didn't want to discourage his daughter. Finally he convinced her to place each ear she picked into a special basket he left at the end of the row he was harvesting. To get to her special basket, Martha had to walk to the end of the row each time she pulled down a new ear of corn, and Matthew could continue to work on his own until she returned to his side.

Fortunately, Mary was able to join them for the harvest. She still had to care for Matthew's infant son. But like her own mother and grandmother before her, Mary simply strapped the boy to her back with his head just above her left shoulder, leaving her two hands free to gather in the harvest. The boy seemed to be happy with this arrangement. He could watch her work or look at his father or follow birds as they flew over the fields.

Matthew and Paul spent each afternoon back in the boatyard where Jacob continued to work on his own while they were in the fields. Paul and Jacob concentrated on finishing the barge they'd been building before Captain Comfort interrupted their work. Matthew turned his attention to building a new sailing canoe to replace the one he'd given to Thomas Hagleton.

By early October, Paul and Matthew were ready to begin their new venture. Each would sail north to a different part of the Bay in search of planters willing to sell them their cured tobacco next spring and to sell their surplus corn and grain the following fall. Matthew would cross over to the eastern side of the Bay and work his way north until he reached the Susquehanna River. Paul would follow the west coast of the Bay north until he reached the Patapsco River, and then he'd head east and north until he came to the Susquehanna.

As Paul launched his canoe out into South River, he felt the excitement of this new venture. This sail was the first time he'd gone alone out to the Bay for a long journey. Now he was a free man and Matthew's partner. He'd be meeting tobacco planters and conducting business with them. The warm air felt wonderful on his face as he entered the Bay and turned north, confident in his sailing skills and eager to make the new venture a success.

On Matthew's advice, Paul sailed past the Severn where he didn't expect to gain any commitments from the Puritan planters who owned most of the land. The name DaSilva still wasn't welcome there. But Paul was surprised and disappointed from his experience on the Magathy. At each plantation where he stopped, he was greeted warmly at first and welcomed in for at least a drink of cider and sometimes a meal. Strangers were a special occasion for these isolated families, who hoped a visitor might bring news of the outside world or of events in other parts of the colony.

But when Paul turned the conversation to trade in tobacco, corn, and grain, he encountered resistance and even hostility. At first he thought these experienced planters didn't want to do business with him due to his age. So he added that he was making the inquiries on behalf of Matthew DaSilva, the senior partner in their venture. He quickly learned that even on the Magathy, the DaSilva name was not welcome.

These early disappointments did not dampen Paul's enthusiasm. Matthew had told him he'd receive a warm welcome from planters when he arrived on the Patapsco. Many of these men still remembered Jose, who had purchased beaver pelts from them and had helped them establish peace with the greatly feared Susquehannock.

Matthew's words proved true when Paul reached the lands of Thomas Sparrow at the mouth of the Patapsco. Sparrow insisted Paul spend the night in his home. He welcomed the opportunity to trade his tobacco and surplus food for the sugar, molasses, cloth, and tools Paul and Matthew would secure from Captain Comfort. Over the years since he'd sold beaver pelts to Jose, Sparrow had grown to be one of the largest and wealthiest landowners in the area. He was so successful, Lord Baltimore had appointed him to serve on his Privy Council. In addition to his own tobacco and surplus food, Sparrow agreed to gather together tobacco, corn, and grains from other planters in the area. Paul left his stay on Sparrow's plantation with renewed optimism.

Although he now had the promise of ample supplies from the area and could start sailing east toward the Susquehanna River, Paul decided he'd try to find Thomas Hagleton while he was here on the Patapsco. Sparrow remembered Hagleton, who had stopped on his lands several months earlier. He told Paul that he'd heard of Hagleton as settling further to the west, just beyond where William Fellson had his wharf. All Paul had to do was to stop at Fellson's wharf and inquire about the blacksmith.

Locating the blacksmith was as easy as Sparrow had indicated. After tying his canoe to Fellson's wharf and greeting the wharf's owner, Paul learned that Hagleton had set up his blacksmith shop in a small shed on the edge of Fellson's property.

Hagleton greeted Paul as if the young man was a long lost member of his family. Paul could see that the man had found a good place to begin his new life.

Hagleton explained that he was renting the shed from Fellson and was using it not only for his blacksmith shop but also as a place to eat and sleep until he could build a house on nearby land that Fellson was willing to sell to him. It was obvious that Hagleton already had a good deal of business established in his small shed. As he and Paul talked, several men stopped by to inquire about tools that Hagleton was forging for them or to order some piece of iron hardware for their home.

At midday, William Fellson came to the shed and invited Paul and Thomas to come to his home for a meal. Fellson talked positively about Thomas and the contribution he was making to their small community.

Having a blacksmith among them solved many problems for the planters. There was now so much traffic to the shed and the wharf that Fellson was thinking about building a small inn on another part of his property.

As they ate their midday meal, Fellson questioned Paul about his journey to the area and how he came to be sailing out here at the far end of the Bay. He showed a great deal of interest in the idea that Paul and Matthew, whom he remembered from his earlier dealings with Jose, would be trading needed goods for the area's tobacco and surplus food. But he showed his strongest interest when Paul began to describe the new type of sailing craft he and Matthew were planning to build for their trading venture.

"You must stop again at my wharf next spring," Fellson told Paul, "when you have one of these new sailing crafts completed. I'm most interested in this new design. It's a long journey from here to St. Mary's City, and even our largest sailing canoes don't carry enough people or cargo to make the trip very productive. If your craft is as large as you say, you'll be able to sell any number of them to planters in this area."

Both Hagleton and Fellson pressed Paul to stay the evening with them. But Paul was eager to get under way again and begin his journey north and east toward the Susquehanna. On the way into the mouth of the Patapsco, he'd seen several islands just off the shoreline on the route up towards the Susquehanna. He'd use the remainder of this day to sail to one of them and stay there overnight. Then he'd make contact with other planters the next day on his way to meet up with Matthew.

30

Surprise on the Susquehanna

Paul awoke on the island, listening to the sounds around him. The sun was rising across the water to the east, bouncing its early morning light across the waves. The wind blew through the pine branches overhead. To his left a squirrel raced across the ground and scampered up the side of a tree. In the distance a woodpecker began its daily search for insects, tapping out a rapid rhythm as it plunged its beak into the bark of a tree.

Paul lay back in the bed of pine needles where he had gone to sleep the evening before.

I'm alone, he thought. For the first time in my life I'm alone. And I'm free. Freedom—it's a wonderful word. If I wanted, I could stay on this island forever. Then again, freedom's just a word. If I stayed here forever, I'd never see Rebecca and Matthew and Mary and Martha again. Freedom means little without family and friends. And now I have both.

With these thoughts running through his head, Paul rose from his island bed and began getting ready for his sail to the Susquehanna. He was pleased with his success along the Patapsco. He hoped he'd have more success as he sailed along the northern edge of the Bay.

About a half hour past the island, he stopped at a small river that the locals called the Gunpowder. The first three planters he met at the mouth of the river agreed to sell him their tobacco and surplus corn when Paul explained how he and Matthew would sail right up to their plantations and save them the work of carrying their crops out to the English ships that anchored out in the Bay each year.

Further along the river he found a very tiny village called Joppatown that had its own wharf, a small inn, and several houses nearby. Those planters had a ship's captain who came each year to buy their tobacco. But they were eager to sell Paul their extra corn. With the price of tobacco going down for the past several years, they welcomed another source of income. Some even suggested they might plant more corn if Paul proved to be a reliable buyer.

As he sailed back out to the Bay, Paul felt confident he and Matthew would have more than enough tobacco and corn from these northern plantations to fill Captain Comfort's ships each season. Now, he thought, it's time to find Matthew and get back to South River so we can begin building our new sailing craft that will make it all work.

Entering the mouth of the Susquehanna, Paul caught sight of Matthew's new sailing canoe pulled up on the land on the east side of the river. He hoped Matthew had been as successful during his sail up the eastern shore of the Bay. But if not, Paul knew he had enough sources of tobacco and corn between Sparrow's land and the Susquehanna to fill Captain Comfort's holds.

Paul lowered his sail and began rowing the final quarter mile to where Matthew had left his canoe. As he came closer, he heard Matthew's voice calling out to him. "What took you so long, partner?" cried Matthew with something of a laugh in his voice. "I've been telling the people of this area about the young man who designs new things in his dreams. They're not sure if you're a magician or just a tall tale I've created to entertain them."

From his words, Paul knew Matthew had been successful too. He rowed a little faster to the shore. There was so much to talk about with his partner. "Matthew," said Paul as he climbed out of his canoe into the shallow water and dragged the craft to the water's edge, "you're well remembered on the Patapsco. Thomas Sparrow has promised us all the tobacco and corn he can raise in a year, and will talk with other planters about selling us their tobacco, grain and corn. I've found other planters who want to trade with us too as I sailed to meet you here. And William Fellson is interested in our new sailing craft. He believes we can sell any extra we build to planters along the Patapsco."

Matthew smiled as he heard the excitement in his young partner's voice. He reached out and gently placed his hand on Paul's shoulder. "Your news is good. I too have had some success. Although almost every planter along the eastern side of the Bay already has a tobacco merchant or ship's captain who takes their tobacco, this area around the Susquehanna should become a bountiful source of corn and grain. Since the time my father visited these shores, many families from a place called Germany have settled along both banks of the Susquehanna. These men are hard working farmers. They're more interested in raising corn, wheat, and other grains than tobacco.

"My friends here think these farmers will welcome a market for what they raise. It will be easy for them to send their crops to us down this river. If there's as much corn and grain as they say, we'll have to build a warehouse right here. That way we can buy their crops and sell them sugar and molasses as well as cloth and tools."

"That's great news," said Paul. "Now let's return to South River so we can begin building the new craft we'll need. If we start right away, we can build at least two new sailing crafts to gather next year's tobacco shipments."

"Not so fast, young friend. It's a long sail back and the day has grown late. Besides, before we climb back into our canoes, there's someone important I want you to meet. Come with me to that house by the stream."

"Alright," said Paul, but he didn't understand why Matthew wanted to delay their departure. It was a long sail back to South River. If they started right now they could sail back to the island where Paul had spent the night and then reach their home well before the sun set on the next day.

Matthew said nothing until they reached the house by the stream. "Wait here, Paul. I'll be right back." Without pausing for a reply, Matthew entered the house. In less than a minute he came back out, followed by a young woman. "Paul, this is Abigail, my new wife! She's the daughter of a man who was one of my father's best friends here on the Susquehanna. When I last saw Abigail she was still playing on the floor while her mother cooked at the fireplace. When I called on her father I was surprised to see that she has become a grown woman."

For a moment, Paul didn't know what to say. He just looked at the young woman and then at Matthew.

"Come now, Paul. I've told Abigail that you're a young man full of many fine ideas who can't stop talking. If you don't say anything now, she'll think I didn't tell the truth and that my partner may be deaf and dumb."

Matthew's gentle rebuke made Paul realize he must appear foolish to this young woman. "I'm most pleased to meet you, Abigail," he stammered. "Forgive my silence. Like Matthew, you are a surprise to me too. But if the smile on

Matthew's face is any indication of how you affect him, then I must say you are the most welcome surprise to come into his life since…" And then Paul stopped.

Several moments of painful silence surrounded Paul, Abigail, and Matthew. Paul didn't know what to say. He felt hot and uncomfortable. His eyes darted from Abigail's face to Matthew and back to Abigail again. Finally Matthew broke the tension.

"That's alright, Paul. Abigail knows I lost Susan to sickness less than 12 months ago. There were deaths here too. She also knows she'll become the mother of two young children when she comes to live with us on South River. You see now why I wasn't ready to set sail with you right away. We'll be bringing Abigail back with us and carrying her possessions in our canoes."

"Paul," said Abigail, "I already can see why Matthew holds you so dear to his heart. When he talks about you, it sounds like he's describing a brother. And if you allow me, I'll greet you in that spirit and think of you from this day forward as my husband's brother."

"Matthew," continued Abigail, "let me introduce Paul to my family. They've prepared a meal for us and have a place where Paul can sleep this night so we can make an early departure tomorrow. I have all of our possessions packed and ready for our journey to my new home on South River. So let us celebrate this evening and then depart with the first light of morning."

Abigail sounds as strong as Mary, thought Paul. I see Matthew welcomes such strength in his new wife. He's not stopped smiling since I came to this shore.

31

Winter on South River

Winter came early to South River. The days turned bitterly cold before the leaves were off the trees. The first snow fell in the second week of November. More snow fell almost every week to the end of the year. The land went to sleep under a thick white blanket. But Paul didn't mind. His daily treks to the stream for water and to the boatyard with Matthew established a path through the snow. And life in the DaSilva household took on a pace that left little time to think about winter.

Paul and Matthew spent every possible hour working in the boatyard. Matthew and Jacob continued to build two barges for local planters. Paul began to carve out sections for the new sailing vessel they'd build based on what they'd learned from the *Deliverance*. He could almost see the new craft taking shape in his mind. His excitement grew as the parts began to emerge out of the wood he cut and shaped each day.

When Matthew wasn't working with Jacob, he was busy making other arrangements for their new business venture. He hired his tenants to cut as many oaks as possible for the new warehouse and wharf they'd construct in the spring. He also spent several days in the forest cutting down cedar trees to use as the pilings they'd set in the river bottom to support the wharf. Every day one of the tenants and Matthew's ox would haul three or four logs to a pile of oak and cedar growing on the side of the boatyard.

Mary and Abigail were busy inside the cabin. They worked well together. Mary was pleased that Matthew had found a new wife, a woman more than eager to raise Martha and the baby. Abigail was grateful for the warm welcome Mary extended to her. She was careful to leave the running of the cabin in Mary's capable hands and to take on the role of her assistant in everything that didn't involve the children.

Both women found their energies and patience taxed to the limit by Martha! At the end of her first evening in the cabin, Abigail rose from the table to take the children up to the sleeping rooms. Holding the baby under one arm, she reached out to take Martha by the hand.

Martha took two steps away from Abigail and declared, "I want this woman to go home to her own family now. She's not my mother. I don't want her here."

Abigail stood still with the baby in her arms, surprised by the vehemence in Martha's words. Mary too remained silent, just looking at her angry granddaughter. No one moved. Finally Matthew stood up and walked over to his daughter, leaned down, and picked her up in her arms. "It's time for you to go to your sleeping room. Abigail is part of our family now. She'll stay with the baby and me in our sleeping room. You'll stay with Mary." With that he carried Martha up to Mary's sleeping room without another word.

The next day Martha made it clear she'd not changed her mind about Abigail. When her father left for the boatyard, again she looked at the young woman defiantly. "It's time for you to go to your own home now!"

This time Mary came to Abigail's rescue. "Martha, last night you heard from your father that Abigail is part of our family. Now I'm going to tell you the same thing. She's not your mother. But she's here to care for you, your brother, and your father. Hold your tongue and don't speak ill to Abigail again." Martha defiantly glared back at her grandmother. Her little hands were clinched in fists. But she held her tongue. Finally she stalked off to a corner of the room to play with wooden blocks Paul had carved for her.

Mary and Abigail knew they'd have to work hard to turn Martha's anger into acceptance. It would be a battle of wills. But at least it was the two of them against one very stubborn child.

By early March, Paul and Matthew could survey their progress with great satisfaction. Jacob was trained to build the barges on his own. Matthew had hired another man to assist him in that work. Freed from building barges, Matthew joined Paul in building the new sailing craft.

The two men slowly assembled the first craft. It was a process of trial and error. They had to stop many times to decide how to join the various sections into a strong framework and hull. Several times they had to take apart a section to make it stronger. Fitting the oak planks in place was more difficult than they'd expected. They learned that any error in setting the first row of planks would be amplified with each successive row.

As Captain Comfort had predicted, the lessons learned building the first sailing craft made the work of the second go much faster. When it was time to set out new tobacco seedbeds, Matthew and Paul had two new sailing crafts ready to test on the river. "We need a name for these new crafts," declared Matthew. "They're not barges of the type we've been building. They're too small to be called ships. They're too large to be called canoes. They look more like one of the rowing skiffs that the English carry with them on their ships, only broader across the beam and with a mast and sail."

"Let's call them sailing skiffs," suggested Paul. "By their lines I expect they'll sail better than our canoes. By their size, they'll carry more cargo than our barges. On the first warm day, we'll test them on the river to see if they are indeed worthy of the name."

"That day best come soon. In less than a week, you and I must sail north to gather the tobacco Captain Comfort expects to load when he arrives here from England. Before we go, I must get the men to start building the new wharf and the warehouse. We'll need both completed by the time we return from our first trading journey north."

"I can't believe this day has arrived so soon," added Paul. "Everything in my life has changed over the past year. I only wish…" he started to say, but then stopped.

"Are you thinking about Rebecca?" asked Matthew. "She's been in my thoughts too. When we return from this first journey for Captain Comfort and we've seen his ship loaded with our first cargo, then you and I will travel back to Battle Town. We'll have made enough from our tobacco trading and the boatyard to meet all of our needs for the coming year and still have money left over. I propose we use some of those funds to purchase Rebecca's freedom from Thomas Cosgrove. If you agree, then we'll travel back to Battle Creek before summer."

Paul looked at Matthew. He was amazed. Had his partner read his thoughts? Did he know Paul's dreams?

32

Returning to Battle Creek

SPRING 1675 — The plantation owners on South River were transplanting their tobacco seedlings into their fields under the warm May sun when Captain Comfort sailed the *Deliverance* up to the new wharf Matthew had constructed for their joint venture. As soon as the *Deliverance*'s mooring lines were secure, Jacob, Matthew, and Paul began rolling the 600 pound hogsheads filled with cured tobacco leaf out of the new warehouse and down on to the wharf. "You've done well," cried out Captain Comfort from the deck of the *Deliverance*. "My sailors can begin filling our hull right away. If you've been able to secure enough good leaf to fill that warehouse, we may be sailing on tomorrow's early tide."

"You'll have enough fine leaf to fill your ship this day," called back Matthew. "And we already have orders for all the cloth, tools, rope, and household goods you can leave with us. When you return in September with sugar and molasses from Barbados, we'll have the warehouse filled with corn and grains from those planters and farmers now settled up and down the Susquehanna. So plan to dine with my family this evening and enjoy some fresh foods and the wonderful cooking of my mother, for you'll be back on the Bay by this time tomorrow."

As Matthew predicted, the *Deliverance* had a short stay on South River. Captain Comfort departed on the early morning tide with a full cargo of tobacco leaf and great confidence in his new partners.

Three days after Captain Comfort sailed down the Bay, Matthew and Paul were ready to set out in their new sailing skiff to Battle Town to buy Rebecca's freedom from her master. Paul was so excited he could barely sleep the night before their departure. Finally, he thought, I can keep my promise to Rebecca. Finally I can provide a home where she'll be safe and secure. As he fell asleep, he dreamed of the surprise on her face when he'd tell her she was free and coming back to South River to be part of the DaSilva household.

"We'll go directly to the Punch to find Thomas Cosgrove," announced Matthew as they sailed past the *Providence* resting quietly at anchor in Battle Creek and headed toward the Battle Town wharf. "When we get there, you go inside to explain our plan to Rebecca while I work out the payment for her freedom. I want to conclude this business as quickly as possible. Have Rebecca gather her possessions so we can be back to the wharf and under sail within the hour."

Cosgrove was standing in front of his inn talking with several men when Paul and Matthew approached him. "What are you doing here in Battle Town, DaSilva? You should know you're not welcome here. Taney told us of your treachery. Any man who helps a slave escape is a traitor to our way of life."

Paul could hear the malice in Cosgrove's voice, but following Matthew's instructions, he slipped around the group and went inside the inn to find Rebecca and get her ready for their journey to South River.

"I'm here only to conduct business with you, sir," replied Matthew.

"What business do you think you have with me?"

"I'm here to purchase your indentured servant, Rebecca."

"And why do you think I'll sell that lazy girl to you?"

"Because I'm willing to pay you a fair price for her purchase. And my payment will be in solid English sterling, not tobacco or goods of any kind."

"Sterling you say," said Cosgrove, surprised that this simple boat builder should have English coins so seldom seen in the colonies. "If you have such coins, I'll sell her to you if the price is right. What do you offer?"

The other men, who'd been talking with Cosgrove, left Matthew and the innkeeper to conduct their business. Now that they were alone, Cosgrove didn't seem so hostile. "I'll offer you five pounds sterling," Matthew said. "That's one pound more than what you provided to Captain Darby under the terms of your original purchase."

"It's been three years since I purchased her from Darby. That means I own her services for eight more years under the laws of this colony. If you calculate my payments to Darby at two pounds per year, then you should pay me at least sixteen pounds sterling for this girl," replied Cosgrove with an edge to his words.

"You purchased her services for five years under the terms of her indenture," said Matthew. "On what basis do you claim payment for eight more years?"

"Taney tells us you serve as one of the local judges back on South River," noted Cosgrove. "Then you should know in this colony we own any young child who's indentured until she reaches the age of 22. Rebecca was 11 when I purchased her service. By my calculations, the law allows me to own her service for 11 years. I've paid the captain for three years and must pay him for two more. If you want to purchase her now from me, I demand full payment for the eight years she owes me under our laws."

"You twist the laws of England and this colony with your logic, Thomas Cosgrove." To Matthew's surprise and the shock of the innkeeper, the voice came from Captain Darby who'd been listening to their conversation from the door of the Punch. "I was inside your inn when Paul entered just now. I greeted him and learned he's come to purchase Rebecca from you. By our contract, you only have rights to two more years because you signed an indenture for five."

Captain Darby smiled at the innkeeper, masking the dislike he'd developed for this man for his harsh treatment of Rebecca.

"The rule of service until 22 only applies to children taken into service without a contract. You, sir, signed a contract for five years with me. I suggest you accept this man's generous offer of five pounds sterling. If I have to testify before a court convened to hear this case, I'm sure the judges will not offer you that extra one pound when they hear my testimony."

Cosgrove stared hard at Darby, but said nothing for several minutes. Then he turned to Matthew. "Show me the five pounds now and I'll release this girl to you."

Matthew quickly reached into the pocket of his coat and withdrew a cloth bag of coins.

"Here's your payment. And thank you for your honest words, Captain Darby. Now innkeeper, please step out of my way so I can leave this place with Paul and his sister."

Cosgrove stood his ground, looking at Matthew with a sneer on his face. "Not so fast, boat builder. The men of Battle Creek still have some business to settle with you."

"What do you mean?"

"Turn around and find out for yourself. I'll let our high sheriff, Michael Taney, explain."

"You'll not leave Battle Town this day, boat builder." It was the voice of Michael Taney, who'd come up behind Matthew with two other men. "You may have finished the business here, but the planters of this area haven't finished with you."

"What do you mean? I'm a free man and free to leave this place with Paul and Rebecca."

"Those two are free to go now that you've paid Cosgrove," said Taney with a dark smile. "But as high sheriff, I arrest you for breaking the laws of this colony. We'll hold your trial this day, here in the inn, and place you in our jail for the next year as punishment for your crime."

"I've committed no crime," protested Matthew. "But by your words, you've already arrested me, tried me, and are ready for my punishment. Yet I've heard no charge against me."

"Then here is your charge and here is your crime. I charge you with marriage to one Abigail of Susquehanna, a white woman born to English parents here in this colony. As an African, you've broken our laws that prohibit marriage of men of your race to white women. Do you deny you've married this white woman?"

"I do not deny it. But I deny that I'm African. I was born here in this colony as the son of a free man and a free woman. I have broken no laws."

"We're a lawful community," said Taney with a mocking tone in his voice. "I'm just the high sheriff, charged with placing you under arrest. It will be up to Thomas Cosgrove and the other judges here with me to hear your claims and then to find you guilty and order your punishment."

"If these men are the judges, then I tell them now that I'm not African. This law doesn't apply to me. My father was Jose DaSilva, a man indentured to the Jesuit Fathers who came here on the Dove, served his indenture, earned his freedom, and was licensed by Lord Baltimore to trade in beaver pelts. Jesuit Fathers baptized my mother as a Catholic. I was born to her in their home on the Severn."

"Did you not tell a court on the South River that your father, this Jose DaSilva, was an African?" asked Taney.

"I did say he was an African. I told the truth, and also said that he was a free man who served the colony and the Calvert family loyally until he died. As the son of a free man and a free woman, I too am a free man."

"The judges will make that decision," sneered Taney.

Finding himself trapped by the high sheriff, Matthew turned to Captain

Darby. "Good captain, tell Paul what's happening here and that he can't help me in this town. Tell him to leave right away and sail back to South River. He should bring Rebecca there and tell Captain Burdett, who's a member of Lord Baltimore's Privy Council and a judge of the Provincial Court, what the men of Battle Town are doing to me."

"Let these children leave as the boat builder says," added Taney. "We have our prisoner. Now we'll have our trial."

33

FATTI MASCHII • PAROLE FEMINE

A Trial in St. Mary's City

Matthew sat with Mary and Captain Burdett in Lord Baltimore's Provincial Court in St. Mary's City. The room was spacious and filled with light from the eight large windows facing south. The furniture was simple by English standards. But it was solidly built of native hardwoods. Elegant, expensive cloth covered each of the chairs set out for the judges. Large oil portraits of the Calvert family looked out over the room, giving the entire space the formal, official feeling appropriate for the colony's highest court.

Three weeks had passed since Matthew's arrest and trial. Matthew considered those days in Battle Town's jail to be the hardest of his young life. I'm not a man who can tolerate locked doors and shackles on my ankles, he thought, as he waited for the judges to appear. He knew he'd shocked his mother when she first saw him enter the courtroom. He felt exhausted by his imprisonment. He'd lost more weight than his lean body could tolerate by refusing to eat the wretched food brought to him in the jail. Now he wondered whether he'd return there for another forty-nine weeks after this new trial. His mind kept asking: will it be prison or freedom? His fate rested on the judgment of these Provincial Court justices who'd hear his case.

As Matthew anticipated, when Paul told his mother and Captain Burdett about his arrest, they understood immediately what to do. His fate rested on an appeal to the governor and his highest court. As a member of the Governor's Privy Council, Captain Burdett was in the best position to make the appeal. He and Mary quickly sailed to St. Mary's City to personally petition the governor on Matthew's behalf. After considering the request for several weeks, Governor Calvert finally ordered Matthew's release and transport to St. Mary's City.

Michael Taney also was in the meeting room, accompanied by two men that Matthew didn't recognize. Captain Burdett identified them as Baker Brooke and Francis Perkins, also members of the Privy Council who'd serve as judges for this hearing. They were waiting for Phillip Calvert, the uncle of the current Lord Baltimore, who'd preside over the Provincial Court on his nephew's behalf.

The side door of the room opened, and in walked Paul with Thomas Sparrow. "When I heard of your arrest and the charges against you," said Burdett to Matthew, "I instructed Paul to sail north to the Patapsco and petition Thomas Sparrow to sail with him to St. Mary's City. Sparrow is a member of the Privy Council. He's entitled to sit as one of your judges."

Phillip Calvert, a distinguished-looking man much older than any of the others in the courtroom, followed Paul and Thomas Sparrow into the room. "I see we're all assembled," noted Calvert, as he moved to the front of the room where a long table stood with five tall-backed chairs behind it.

"Mister Sparrow, Captain Burdett, please join me here at the judges' table. Mister Brooke, Mister Perkins, it is good to see you here also. I hope your travels here from the Patuxent were pleasant. Please join me at the judges' table too."

The elder Calvert examined a few papers an aide had placed on the desk in front of his chair and waited for the other judges to take their seats. Finally he looked up, cleared his voice and began the proceedings.

"I serve as the senior justice at the pleasure of Lord Baltimore," announced Calvert in a strong, clear voice that rang with authority. "Mister Taney, as high sheriff, you've brought charges against this man, Matthew DaSilva. Please explain the charges to the court and why the judges in Battle Town found him guilty of a crime against the laws of this colony."

"Thank you, your lordship," intoned Taney in a most respectful voice. "The charge is simple. The evidence is clear. This man, an African, has married one Abigail of Susquehanna, a white woman born to English parents here in the colony. Matthew DaSilva testified in one of your courts that his father was an African. He confirmed the truth of that heritage at his trial in Battle Town. Our judges found him guilty of breaking the law of this colony that no African shall marry a white woman. He's affirmed his marriage to this woman, Abigail. On the basis of this marriage, he's been found guilty and sentenced to a year in jail."

"On what basis do you, Matthew DaSilva, make your appeal and contest these words of the high sheriff?" asked Calvert.

Matthew stood, bowed to the judges, and glanced quickly toward Mary and Paul before addressing the court.

"I thank you, your lordship, for convening this hearing," replied Matthew in a voice as respectful as Taney's. "I also thank Lord Baltimore for granting me this appeal. I do not dispute the facts as the high sheriff has presented them. But he has made a claim that I am an African. That claim is not true. The judges in Battle Town would hear no evidence from me. Today I will prove them wrong."

"I'm the son of Jose DaSilva, a man of African descent who came to this colony in 1632 aboard the Dove, one of the two ships sent by your brother to establish the first settlement here in St. Mary's City. Jose was born of a Portuguese father and an African mother. He came here indentured to the Jesuit Fathers. He served them well for five years and gained his freedom. He then secured a permit to enter the trade in beaver pelts and pursued that work until his death. I repeat these facts for the benefit of your lordship and the other esteemed judges."

"Now if it pleases your lordship, I'll introduce the evidence that proves my innocence. In this room sits my mother, Mary, who was born in this colony on the eastern shore of the Chesapeake, to parents who were part of the Nanticoch peoples. She was captured as a child and taken as a slave by Susquehannock warriors. My father, Jose, purchased her freedom from those people when he was trading with them for beaver pelts. He brought her here, to St. Mary's City, to be baptized as a Catholic by the Jesuit Fathers. As a member of our faith and the wife of a free man, Mary also is a free woman under the laws of the colony.

Matthew paused, scanning the faces of the five judges to gauge the impact of his words. He knew the next part of his argument would be central to winning this appeal. He waited a moment longer, making sure he had the full attention of each judge.

"I was born to Mary on the Severn River. As the son of a free woman who was born to the people of the Nanticoch, I claim that my heritage is not African. No man knows the true identity of his father. Everyone knows the identity of his mother. While I do claim that Jose was my father, and I carry his name and honor his memory, I claim my heritage from my mother under the laws and practice of England and this colony. For this reason I am not an African. I am a free man, and my marriage to Abigail does not violate any law."

The chief judge looked to his colleagues on his left and on his right. "Do any of my fellow justices have questions of these two men?" He paused briefly before starting his questions of the four powerful men who would decide Matthew's fate. "Do any of you dispute the claims this man's made about his father and mother?"

Again the chief justice paused, and again he turned his head and looked at each of the judges in turn. Getting no responses to his questions and no reactions to his gaze, a slight smile appeared on his face. He let the silence fill the room for another brief moment. Then he broke the rising tension in the room.

"Gentlemen, hearing no questions or refutation of these claims, I'll ask for your judgments. Mister Brooke, what's your verdict?"

"I find this man, Matthew DaSilva, to be guilty as charged. Under the laws of England and this colony, we gain our inheritance from our fathers. He's admitted his father was an African. Therefore, I judge him also to be an African. As such he has broken our laws on marriage of Africans to white women."

"Thank you, Mister Brooke, for your careful reasoning," said the chief justice. And what is your judgment, Mister Perkins?"

"I concur with Judge Brooke. I'll add that the law prohibiting such marriages has been in effect for more than a decade here in Maryland. It also states that any child born to a slave also becomes a slave for life, and that should a white woman marry an African, then any of her children become slaves. I find Matthew DaSilva guilty for marrying a white woman, and therefore, any children from this marriage will become slaves."

"Thank you gentlemen," replied the chief justice, who looked out across the large table, first at Matthew, and then at Mary. His eyes locked on each of them for almost a minute. The chief justice's smile was no longer apparent, but no other emotion had taken its place.

"And what is your judgment, Captain Burdett?"

"With all due respect for my esteemed colleague and friend," began the captain, taking an extra moment to acknowledge the other judge seated to his left, "I find the reasoning of Judge Brooke to be in error. While it's true our laws specify that a son inherits his property from the father, my fellow judge is confusing inheritance with heritage. English law has long recognized that every child receives lineage and heritage from the mother, and with good cause. The mother is known with certainty. The true identity of the father may be in question. Matthew DaSilva's heritage comes from his mother. She is a good Catholic, born here in Maryland. Therefore Matthew is not an African. He's the son of a free woman of Nanticoch heritage. As a free man born to a free woman, he's not broken our laws by his marriage to Abigail."

The chief justice nodded to Captain Burdett, letting his words in defense of Matthew linger in the air before proceeding.

"And what say you, Mister Sparrow?"

"I agree with the point that Captain Burdett has made, and I'll point out another error in the argument for a guilty verdict. Our laws that prohibit marriages are written to prohibit the marriage of a slave to a white woman. Judge Perkins has substituted the word African for the word slave. Although all our slaves are Africans, it is not true that all Africans are slaves. No one has claimed that Jose DaSilva was a slave. Such a claim would be false. Jose became a free man, and therefore his son, Matthew, also must be a free man. As a free man whose heritage comes from his mother, he has broken no law."

Matthew felt a sense of relief as he listened to the strength of his friends' arguments. But he knew the trial was not yet done. Everything now depended on the decision of the chief justice, to whom Matthew now looked for some sign of his reactions to the four arguments placed before the court. Worry seized Matthew again when he found no hint or clue on the chief justice's face.

"We have two judges prepared to find this man guilty," commented the chief justice in a firm and commanding voice. "Two find him innocent. That leaves the final decision to me." Chief Justice Calvert again paused for a moment. Then he slowly looked at the two justices to his left and the two justices to his right. Finally, he looked out again at Matthew and Mary. Still no emotion showed on his face.

"Wise arguments have been made in favor of finding this man guilty. Other wise arguments have been made that would find him innocent. I thank each of my fellow judges for the care and thought they have given to this case."

The chief justice locked his eyes on Matthew.

"With the greatest respect to my two colleagues, Baker Brooke and Francis Perkins, I find the law applies as has been stated by Captain Burdett and Thomas Sparrow. This man is neither an African nor a slave. He is a free man whose heritage comes from his mother. As such, he has committed no crime through his marriage to Abigail. Matthew DaSilva," said the chief justice, "I grant you your appeal and find you innocent of these charges. Your freedom is restored."

"But note carefully, Matthew DaSilva, it's the opinion of this court that high sheriff Taney acted properly and with cause in bringing these charges against you, as witnessed by opinions of two of the most highly respected justices of this court. You have no grounds for action against the high sheriff or any of the judges who convicted you in Battle Town. I now declare this hearing before the Provincial Court to be closed."

With that statement, Phillip Calvert rose from the judges' table and walked out of the court. Baker Brooke and Francis Perkins followed close behind the chief justice. When Michael Taney walked past Matthew on his way to the door, he paused.

"You may be free by action of this court, boat builder, but you're not free from future retribution from those you've injured. There are crimes before the law, and there are crimes before the people. Both bring their proper punishments in time."

Matthew said nothing in reply. He understood the threat in Taney's words, but they could not wipe away the joy and relief he felt as he placed his arms around Mary and Paul.

When Taney had left the room, he turned to Captain Burdett and Thomas Sparrow. "Thank you, good friends, for coming here and speaking in my defense. I dare not think how the chief justice would have ruled if the hearing had been before only three justices, with two of them acting in support of Michael Taney."

"Say no more," replied Captain Burdett. "We all know you'd have been found guilty and would be back in jail for the next year. I know that Phillip Calvert remembers your father as loyal to the Calverts and as a good member of his church. But the power of the Puritans and those like Taney who count themselves as Protestants are now rising against the Catholic Calverts. Lord Baltimore can't afford to make enemies of men like Brooke and Perkins. That's the meaning behind the chief justice's final words to you."

"Have no fear on that account," said Matthew. "I'll make a wide circle around the mouth of the Patuxent when we sail this afternoon back to South River. A wise man doesn't enter a cave filled with poisonous snakes. So let's be gone from here. Thomas Sparrow, will you join us at my home on South River for a celebration. It's a modest cabin, but one where you always will be welcome for your aid and friendship."

"Thank you, Matthew," replied Sparrow. "In memory of Jose and in response to the plea from his fine young fellow, I was more than willing to sail here to your aid. But I've much work to do back on my land. I'll ask you to allow Paul to bring me back to the Patapsco in one of your new sailing skiffs before he joins you back on the South River. That's enough kindness from your household for this day."

"Then it's back to our homes," said Matthew. "Let's be off."

34

Homecoming on South River

As Matthew tied his sailing skiff to his wharf on South River, he saw Jacob walking toward him from the boatyard. "How goes the work?" he called as he climbed up on the wharf. Jacob didn't reply. He continued walking silently toward the skiff. Matthew could see a worried look on his face. "What's wrong? Are Abigail and my children alright?"

"Your wife and children are fine, sir. It's the boatyard. A day after your mother and Captain Burdett sailed to St. Mary's City, there was a terrible fire. The shed's been destroyed. All of the oak planks and maple timbers you'd stored there are gone. The barge we'd finished building has been ruined, and the pine logs we'd prepared for the next two canoes are burned beyond use."

By this time, Mary and Captain Burdett had climbed out of the skiff and were standing next to Matthew. For a moment no one spoke. "How did this happen, Jacob?" asked Matthew. "We use no fire in our work. It makes no sense that everything there should be destroyed."

Before Jacob could answer, Matthew was striding past him toward the boatyard. When he reached the shed, he saw Jacob's description was accurate. The shed was destroyed. Some of the lumber still smoldered. The smell of smoke was everywhere. He could barely look at the blackened remains of the barge and canoes sitting in the work area. Anger grew inside Matthew as he surveyed the destruction. "What about the warehouse and my cabin?"

"Both are safe. I wasn't here when the fire started. It was night. I think it's best you hear the full account from Abigail. She was unable to save your boatyard, but I believe she saved your warehouse, your cabin, and your family."

Mary already had walked past Matthew toward the cabin. Matthew, Captain Burdett, and Jacob followed quickly behind. As they approached their home, they could see Abigail, Rebecca, Martha, and the baby in the small kitchen garden Mary had planted this year just beyond the cabin door.

"Matthew," cried Abigail, "you're safe and home! I've been so worried about you."

"And I about you," replied Matthew. "By what I've seen, you've been in more danger than me. Are you and Rebecca and the children alright?"

"Yes, we're fine. But I wasn't able to save your boatyard."

"That matters little as long as you're safe."

Matthew placed his arms around Abigail, saying nothing more but letting his embrace tell her what his words could not convey. What a strong woman, he thought. I'm so fortunate to have found her.

Suddenly Matthew was aware that Paul and Mary were staring at him. He knew he had to let this moment go and attend to the damage and destruction all around him.

"But what happened? Jacob says you saved our family and what remains of my property."

"It happened after Mary and Captain Burdett sailed to St. Mary's City. I'd just put Martha and the baby down for the night in our sleeping room. As I descended the stairs, Rebecca and I heard shouts coming from the boatyard. We ran to the door to see what was happening.

"We could see fire rising to the sky from your shed. A man was shouting. I saw two or three men in the flickering light of the fire. They seemed to be running about the boatyard with torches. One of them called out, 'Death to the African! Death to the Catholics!' I feared they'd come to the cabin and harm us."

"But Abigail protected us," said Rebecca suddenly. "She ran back into the cabin and came out with your musket. I've never seen a woman fire a musket before. She loaded powder and a musket ball into the barrel, aimed at the men in the boatyard, and fired. Then she loaded the musket again and fired a second time."

Matthew stared at Abigail, not knowing what to say. He watched as a blush of embarrassment rose to her cheeks. She dropped her eyes toward the ground, avoiding Matthew's gaze.

"Now Rebecca," said Abigail, "don't make too much of what happened."

Her eyes darted back toward Matthew, wondering what her husband would make of her story.

"I don't think I hit any of them," added Abigail in a voice so soft Matthew had to struggle to hear her words. "It was a long distance to the yard and it was dark. But I wanted them to know they'd pay dearly if they tried to come to the cabin. The shouting ended then. The men and their torches seemed to run toward the wharf. When I reached the boatyard, they were gone. The fires were burning so strongly we couldn't do anything to save your shed or the canoes."

"I didn't know you could fire a musket, let alone reload and fire again," said Matthew in wonder at his young wife.

Again the blush rose on Abigail's face. Only the concern and respect she sensed in Matthew's words allowed her to continue.

"Growing up on the Susquehanna is not the same as living in St. Mary's City. My father taught me to hold a musket, aim, and shoot when I was just a few years older than Martha. By the time I was Rebecca's age, I could shoot and hunt as well as my brothers."

Abigail could see the pride in Matthew's face. A smile replaced her blush.

"Had it been daylight, one of those men would not have been able to get away. I only regret we don't know who they were."

"I've been asking about them since the fire," added Jacob. "I learned three men came to the inn on the day Mary and the captain left. All three were strangers. One was described as not much older than Paul. He seemed to be their leader. He asked where he could find the man who built barges out of rowing canoes. The man who talked to him said he had the letter T branded on his hand."

Matthew considered Jacob's description, recalling that trial in Battle Town, which now seemed so long ago and far away.

"I suspect Paul and I know this man," said Matthew. "But suspicion is not proof. I've no intention to travel to Battle Creek to find out if he was the one who caused all this damage."

"If your suspicions also take you to Michael Taney," commented Captain Burdett, "I can't blame you. I heard what he said to you as he left the Provincial Court. There's no doubt it was a threat. I just didn't believe he would act in such an evil way."

Matthew stood silently, looking first at his family safely gathered around him and then to the boatyard where his life's work lay in ruin. The fear he felt at the wharf and the anger in the boatyard began to slip away. Doubt and despair took their place. Matthew shook his head. "Now I have to decide what to do."

"Matthew, you're a good man," added Burdett, "and one I count as a friend. So hear what I say as someone who respected your father and welcomed him and his family to South River.

"I believe the planters on the Patuxent have been poisoned with a disease called slavery. They think their fortunes depend on growing tobacco with men they own for life.

"With the price of tobacco half what it was when I first came to this area, it's almost impossible to make a profit with indentured servants. Fewer men and women are willing to leave England for the hard work of raising tobacco.

"The larger plantation owners can afford the higher price for purchasing a slave. They know that owning and working a man for fifteen or twenty or thirty years will bring more profit than paying for five years of labor from an indentured servant.

"I already feel the pressure to bring slaves to South River. Before your daughter grows old enough to marry, there will be slaves throughout this area. You must think about the safety of your family as this poisonous practice spreads throughout the Bay."

"I'd thought my homecoming would give us a chance to celebrate," replied Matthew. "Now that we're here, I find only difficult decisions. I must confess…I don't know what to do."

"Those decisions are not yours alone," said Mary. "Now you have Paul as your partner. He has a voice in the decision too. Let's wait until he returns from the Patapsco. It may be easier to see what to do when you've had some time to think and when Paul's with us again."

A look of relief came over Matthew's face as he turned to his mother. "Your words, mother, are always strong and true. I'm fortunate to have your counsel. We'll wait for Paul. I'll not make my decisions out of fear, or anger, or despair. I need time to let these feelings pass before I face the future."

35

Fateful Decisions

The smell of burned wood hung heavily in the air when Paul tied his sailing skiff to the wharf on South River. He'd expected the boatyard to be busy now that Matthew was free. Instead only silence greeted him. An uneasy feeling gripped him as he climbed out of the skiff. What's happened here, he thought. Who did this? And why?

As these questions ran through his mind, Paul noticed Matthew standing in front of the half-burned shed. "Matthew," he called, "what's happened to your family, and my sister, and our boatyard?"

"Calm yourself," replied Matthew. "All are safe."

Slowly, Matthew recounted the attack and what he'd learned from Abigail and Rebecca. Paul stood speechless as Matthew explained the losses they'd suffered. Almost aimlessly he walked first to the shed, and then around the burned remains of the barge they'd been building. He bent down to feel the ashes of the burnt lumber. Sadness filled his face.

"Matthew," he finally asked, "what should we do?"

"Jacob and I have recovered most of our tools from the shed. The wooden handles are no good, but the iron heads from our axes, adzes, and hatchets are fine and the drawing knives and planes can be rebuilt too. There are ample trees here on South River and on my land on the Severn, and we've the labor to cut the lumber and timbers we'll need to rebuild the shed. We just have to decide if we should begin again."

Paul appreciated the value of what Matthew was saying. With their tools, they could rebuild what had been destroyed. But this news didn't lift the heavy weight he was feeling as they surveyed the damage. Again he asked, "What should we do?"

"Let us go back to the cabin," replied Matthew. "Everyone is looking to us to make those decisions. We'd be fools not to include Mary and Abigail in our council. They'll not force a decision on us. But watch their reactions closely. If they don't show agreement, we'll have to rethink our choices." As the two men approached the cabin, Matthew called to his mother and his wife. "Mary, Abigail, please come out to the yard to join us. It's time to decide what to do. Rebecca, you should come too. Our decisions will affect everyone in this family."

Mary was the first to speak. "What have you decided?"

"I've been thinking a great deal about the words of Captain Burdett," replied Matthew. "I believe he's correct. Slavery will spread throughout this area. Neither Paul nor I like the idea of living where men are slaves. Plantation owners who own slaves will grow to hate us for our views. But I don't like the idea of being driven from our home and lands by men who hate us."

"Neither did your father," answered Mary. "He had your courage and determination to face any danger. But like you, he also had a family. Given the hatred of the Puritans, he choose to leave our home on the Severn and come here to South River."

"I've been thinking of Jose too," said Matthew. "I'm not sure I've his courage. But I do have the good counsel of his wife and my mother. If Paul is willing, I think we should leave this place and head to the north of the Bay. We have the trade with the planters and German farmers who live there. There're still good feelings toward the DaSilva family from the many things Jose did for the early settlers in that area. What do you think, Abigail? Will we find welcome there?"

"We're now part of my family on the Susquehanna too. There're some fine islands at the mouth of the river that are too small for plantations but offer good shelter for a new warehouse and wharf, for our new cabin and these children. I'm sure we'll be welcomed there."

"What say you, Paul?"

"I'm pleased to hear what Abigail says about a new home on the

Susquehanna. I believe we'd be welcomed on the north shore of the Patapsco. Thomas Sparrow is a powerful man and has proven his friendship. William Fellson has land that would serve us well for a new boatyard. By the way I've seen the men in that area welcome Thomas Hagleton, they may have less hatred for Africans. But what will you do with your lands on South River and the Severn if we leave this area, Matthew? We've built a new warehouse and a wharf for our partnership with Captain Comfort. It will be difficult to leave all these things."

"I've given those matters some thought while waiting for you to return. I've good tenants on these lands on South River and on the Severn. I'll offer to sell them the lands they now farm if we can agree on a fair price. I'll not require payment right away, and will take a share of their tobacco harvest each year until they pay their debts to me.

"As to the boatyard, I'll offer it to Jacob. He now knows how to build our Chesapeake Bay barges. He can pay me for the boatyard over several years from the profits he makes from his labors. There's plenty of demand for his work on South River. And when the Puritans on the Severn know I no longer make the barges, they may purchase from him too.

"If Jacob and my tenants don't want these purchases, I'll offer everything to Captain Burdett. He's interested in our warehouse and wharf already. He has the means to buy all that I own in addition if he wants. What say you to this plan, Paul?"

Paul felt the sincerity in Matthew's voice. *He really sees me as his partner,* Paul thought. *And now I have to think about Rebecca and Matthew's entire family too.*

Paul suddenly felt older, knowing for the first time the responsibilities of becoming a man in this new world that had become his home. Slowly he looked around at the faces of the people waiting for his answer. Finally, he knew what to say.

"By the look on Mary's face and the smile from Abigail, I believe, Matthew, you have spoken what's best for us all. How will we decide between the Patapsco and the Susquehanna?"

"It will be best to choose both," replied Matthew. "Here's what I propose. I'll take my family back to Abigail's home on the Susquehanna. When they're safe there, I'll arrange to purchase one of the islands and will pay some men to build a new cabin."

"You, Paul, stay here for now and watch over our warehouse and wharf. When I return, you should sail to the Patapsco and purchase some land either from William Fellson or as close to him and Thomas Hagleton as possible.

Select a good site where we can build our new boatyard. I believe our family will be safest if we have people and property in both locations. You'll be in charge of the boatyard and a new wharf and warehouse on the Patapsco. I'll manage our trading from a new warehouse in the mouth of the Susquehanna. Abigail, what do you say to this plan?"

"I'll do as my husband decides," said Abigail, who could not hide a smile.

"I see the wisdom of your plan," said Paul. "We'll be much safer among these friends and Abigail's family, and have the advantage of building our trading business through both locations. But what about Rebecca?"

"I'll answer that question," replied Mary. "Rebecca and I have already spoken. She'll come with Abigail and me and the children. Paul, your sister needs to live among the women in her family for several years as she becomes a young woman. Matthew, I'll need Rebecca with us when Abigail gives birth to your next child, which should be before the first winter snow if I know anything about this process. When you have those men build our next cabin, make sure they build a home large enough for a very big family. If Abigail is with child so soon, then I expect to have many more grandchildren to comfort me as I grow old."

"Paul," said Matthew with a broad smile on his face, "it appears that most of our important decisions have been made already by the women in this family. So let's get to work and make these things happen before they change their minds."

Epilogue

"**G**randmother Martha," pleaded little Joseph, "please tell us again how thee came to live here on the Susquehanna. And how great-great grandfather Jose came from England with the *Ark* and the *Dove*."

"And tell how thee became the wise healer for all of us," said Mary, his older sister.

"Thee should let thy grandmother rest," scolded their mother, who had been straining to get her children off to bed for the past hour on this warm summer evening. She knew their grandmother loved them dearly. And if they could get her telling the old family history, it would be hours before they'd go to sleep.

"We gather for Meeting tomorrow," said Martha. "I shall need my rest this night. Our Quaker brethren will arrive early and stay late. There are many decisions we must make at our mid-summer gathering. I want thee well rested so thee can sit with us in silent worship all morning."

"Oh, please, just one story," pleaded Mary again.

"Tell us how the first Jose lived with the Susquahannocks and the Nanticokes," added her brother, who never tired of hearing about the original people who had lived on this land. "Tell us about the great storm and the fire in the boatyard and the building of our home and the wharf and the warehouse on our island."

"Enough," said their father as he entered the large kitchen where his family had gathered. "Mother Martha must be well rested for tomorrow. As our most senior Elder, all will look to her counsel as we make decisions for our Meeting."

Martha smiled as she looked at her oldest son, John. He was so much more like his grandfather, Matthew, than her own husband, whose quiet ways and simple language had won her heart and made her conversion to the Quaker faith so easy. Like his grandfather, John was more interested in building sailing skiffs and expanding their trade. He even was talking about building a larger mill so they could ship flour to the colonies in the north rather than just selling the grain they purchased from the farmers on the Susquehanna.

But when it came to the Meeting's quiet deliberations, she knew she could count on John's clear thinking and good counsel. Many of their Quaker brethren were troubled by the decision the Meeting had made last year to help slaves who had escaped from their masters make their journeys north to the safety of Philadelphia. Some argued they were stealing the property of the plantation owners by helping these men and women escape. Others feared the Maryland Assembly would ban their worship as Quakers as punishment. The Meeting would have to spend many hours in thoughtful conversation before these doubts and fears would be resolved. As the senior Elder, she could not force this decision. She had to make sure every member who was troubled by this aid to escaped slaves would have a chance to speak.

In the end, though, she knew that no one would change her mind or the commitment of John to this work. Others in the Meeting might not know the history of her grandfather or the courage of his son when faced with the anger and hostility of the plantation owners who first brought slaves to this colony. But her family would never forget their history and heritage. They'd continue this work. And she knew some day young Mary and Joseph also would stand up for what's right and just.

Praise for *Battle Creek*

"The 17th century is America's forgotten era when settlers lived and died clinging to the edge of a vast new continent. The Chesapeake Bay settlements were a rough and ready world where opportunity called but hardship and death were always present.

Battle Creek captures this world for young readers with a story that cuts to the heart of every settler's dance with fate. Siblings, alone and vulnerable, face a potent mix of danger, ignorance, hard work, evil, kindness, and good luck. The result is a page turning pleasure."

Burt Kummerow
President
Maryland Historical Society

"Never has the settling of Maryland been so convincingly described, with so much emotional impact. Don't be fooled by this remarkable book for young people; it is filled with a pointed way of looking at early Maryland that is not normally available.

"Sympathetically and emotionally alive, Neil Didriksen writes an important complement to scholarship on 17th century Maryland. This book is full of life, detail, and truth. Finally, we have a book that captures what the region's Englishmen and women, Native Americans, and African Americans felt like in the 1670s.

Battle Creek is a needed book."

Mark P. Leone
Professor of Anthropology
University of Maryland, College Park

About the Author

Battle Creek is a first novel for Neil Didriksen, whose professional career spans thirty years in nonprofit marketing and communications. The novel combines Neil's avocation as an amateur historian with his interest in bringing colonial Maryland to life for young readers. When not exploring historical archives, Neil serves as the chief operating officer of a private foundation. He is at work on second and third historical novels set in Maryland for young readers.

Acknowledgments

As a writer intrigued by Maryland's role in America's history, a wonderful team of experts and collaborators has aided me at every stage of my work. Burt Kummerow, Executive Director of the Maryland Historical Society, has been my guide through Maryland's early colonial history. Scott Fuqua has tapped his expertise as an author to serve as my editor. Tom Chalkley's illustrations have given life and vitality to my prose. Amy Morgante has provided thoughtful suggestions and encouragement as she carefully proofed the final text.

Throughout the process, I've been inspired by my two muses, Jane and Daniel.

CITYLIT
PRESS

CityLit Press's mission is to provide a venue for writers who might otherwise be overlooked by larger publishers due to the literary nature or regional focus of their projects. It is the imprint of nonprofit CityLit Project, a literary arts center located in Baltimore.

CityLit Project builds enthusiasm for the literary arts in the Baltimore metropolitan area and across Maryland for the benefit of readers, writers, and diverse audiences of all ages. It presents public festivals, author events, writers workshops, and programs for youth and seniors. It launched the CityLit Press imprint in 2010.

Thank you to major supporters: the National Endowment for the Arts, Maryland State Arts Council, the Baltimore Office of Promotion and The Arts, and the Baltimore Community Foundation. More information and documentation is available at www.guidestar.org.

Additional support is provided by individual contributors. Financial support is vital for sustaining the ongoing work of the organization. Secure, on-line donations can by made at www.citylitproject.org (click on "Donate").

CityLit is a member of Maryland Citizens for the Arts, the Greater Baltimore Cultural Alliance, the Maryland Association of Nonprofit Organizations, and the Writers' Conferences and Centers division of the Association of Writers and Writing Programs (AWP).

CityLit Project's offices are located in the School of Communications Design at the University of Baltimore.